"Are you playing pirate again, Rathe, with your sunken galleon and your lovemaking?"

He stroked her shoulders, his hands moving downward, the bikini top no deterrent to his searching fingers. Sensations of excruciating intensity welled up in her. She desperately wanted him to stop and to go on at the same time.

"I'm not playing at anything, Lorelei, I'm very serious. I want you. I've tried not to but, God help me, I still do."

There was no denying that he wanted her, and that she wanted him. Her breasts tingled with the electricity of desire as they brushed against the hair on his chest.

"My beloved pirate," she murmured.

Second Chance at Love™

BELOVED PIRATE
MARGIE MICHAELS

A JOVE BOOK

First Jove edition published October 1981

First printing

"Second Chance at Love" and the butterfly emblem are trademarks belonging to Jove Publications, Inc.

Printed in the United States of America

Jove books are published by Jove Publications, Inc.,
200 Madison Avenue, New York, NY 10016

CHAPTER ONE

LORELEI AVERILL STARED at the slim, sophisticated young woman, elegantly dressed in her long, sparkling, emerald green skirt and filmy, white silk top and wondered who she was. The long, lustrous black hair was shiningly clean and swirled high on top of her head; her face, familiar and yet unfamiliar, looked exotic with its professionally applied layer of makeup. She felt out of place in the fine feathers.

"Well, well," a voice interrupted her reverie. "What's happened to the greatest tomboy on all the seven seas?" Retired Navy Vice-Admiral Walter Averill looked at his daughter's reflection in the mirror and pronounced a favorable judgment. "You are an arrestingly beautiful woman, Lorelei, and you look just like your mother—rest her soul—did twenty-five years ago!"

Lorelei wrinkled her nose at the reflection to convince herself that the image was her own and not a painted picture of someone else. They were going to a costume ball and she was dressed to look the part of a siren—sensuous, alluring; and though it wasn't meant to be taken seriously, the image before her was so different from the Lorelei Averill she had come to know as herself in the past six years, that she turned away from it and took the drink her father proffered, concentrating on it rather than on the evening ahead.

"I feel like Cinderella going to that very first ball, but somehow I don't think I'll be a fairy-tale vision of elegance." Here mischief lit up her bright green eyes. "I'm going to be supping and dancing with the crème de la crème of high Nassau society and all the time I'll be tripping over my glass slippers."

Her father chuckled appreciatively and moved to ruffle her hair, a habit held over from her childhood, but his hands dropped before they reached that beautiful but untouchable creation and fell to his sides.

"Lorelei, you can't spend the rest of your life guiding tours and sailing around the Bahamas in your rattletrap of a boat. It's time you decommissioned it—and yourself! What would your mother think of your harum-scarum sort of life?"

"She'd probably wonder why you were trying so hard to change it, since you were the one who raised me to enjoy it." She stuck her tongue out at him, ruining the sophisticated image. "I don't see why I have to give up everything I enjoy simply because I'm getting married."

It was an argument they'd had often of late, ever since Stavros Halkias, heir to the Halkias shipping fortune, had proposed and she had accepted.

"Can you see Stavros running his family's shipping business from aboard *your* boat, dressed—like you, I might add—in a baggy tee shirt, cut-off shorts, and a white sailor's cap? You'd look like deck apes, the pair of you, and I guarantee you wouldn't command much respect that way."

"I'm not going to command anything but laughter looking like *this*," she replied, though a certain light in her eyes belied her words. "I'll be making a spectacle of myself."

"A siren is supposed to make a spectacle of herself," he reminded her. "That's the whole idea. Unwary sailors. Why, even the gods themselves are reputed to have crashed onto the rocks, lured there by a siren's song."

Lorelei stifled a laugh. Her father was a notorious storyteller. "If you think for one minute that I can do that, then it's obvious you haven't been listening to me sing in the shower." She continued on a more serious note. "But you know, dad, I'd really rather have announced this engagement my own way and not at such a large gathering, and especially one as formal as the annual masquerade of the poshest marina around. I'm sure that took a lot of finagling, even for Mama Halkias. I'm doing it for Stavros—he's so close to his family, and I know just how pleased they are about their only son's settling down, as you would say. But then who can blame them?" She laughed. "He *did* make an excellent choice!"

"And so did you, Lorelei, so did you," he said approvingly. Lorelei could not help but wonder if she didn't detect a note of relief in her father's voice. For Stavros certainly seemed to be the perfect life mate—mature, gentle, and unselfishly loving. Definitely not like someone else she had known once . . . but quickly she put the thought out of her mind.

"I do wish though, dad," she continued, "that pirates hadn't been chosen as the dance's theme this year."

"Whyever not?" He frowned. "The Bahamas have a long history of pirates. Blackbeard, Charles Vane, William Kidd—they all roamed our islands. I think everyone, native and tourist alike, is rather proud of it."

"Not this one." She handed him a newspaper clipping from an end table. It was a picture of her and one of her tourists. "He was robbed by our resident gang of twentieth-century pirates while exploring one of the outislands. They probably followed him, and they took all his money and his wife's jewelry. I think all the romance died out of that particular legend for him. I realize they didn't hurt him, but it isn't pleasant to be stopped on the high seas. You know how concerned I am about my clients, and I can just hear what they would say if they saw me in tomorrow's paper sporting a pirate on each arm, wielding a cutlass and a sash full of money."

"I'm aware of your feelings for them, Lorelei, and I know that it's your concern in particular that's made your business a success. I also know, however, that if we don't get a move on, Stavros is going to think you've changed your mind." He snapped off the lights and held the door open for her to exit.

After they'd settled in the car and were finally heading for the marina that was to host the dance, Lorelei had a chance to reflect on the events of the past several weeks. How strange a part fate plays in our lives, she thought, and then was forced to smile at the cliché. But then, she considered, wasn't it the truth to be found in clichés that made them so often repeated? For in the normal course of things, the Halkias family would never tarry long in the Bahamas and certainly never maintain one of their many homes here. After all, even she, who so dearly loved the Bahamas, realized they did not rival the beauty of the Greek Islands. But Stavros's only sister had met the son of a wealthy South American family on the slopes of Gstaad, eventually married him, and expanded the Halkias family into the New World. And though his parents were hardly in the Bahamas full time, Stavros himself had found a home here. Though he didn't have to worry about money, he did have to prove to himself that he could become established in a field on the basis of his own skill. That's where his diving came in.

So they met and had been great friends for the past few years, she and Stavros, and they had much in common, making their livelihoods from the sea. He had always treated her with a refreshing Old World charm and courtesy, yet she had never once suspected him of wanting a deeper relationship until, several weeks ago, he had, in the Greek tradition, asked her father for her hand in marriage. Pleasantly surprised, she accepted. She was, after all, twenty-five now, and her father was right— Stavros could offer her the kind of security she needed. Or at least that's what she kept telling herself. She never dared mention to her father or her friends, and rarely even allowed herself to consider the fact that at times she felt just a little unsure about the marriage to the gentle and gentlemanly Stavros. Perhaps, she reflected, if she had never before experienced the passionate, almost electrical rapport that sometimes happens between a man and his woman . . . She pursed her lips in speculation.

"Penny for your thoughts sweetheart?" Her father's concerned voice broke into her thoughts. He took one hand from the wheel to squeeze hers affectionately, seemingly aware of what— or rather of whom—she thought as her coral ring bit into his flesh.

"You should take his ring off now, Lorelei," he counseled her softly. "You'll soon have a much nicer one to replace it with." He tugged at the ring that was tightly fitted to her finger. "I know that Stavros plans to give you a diamond tonight, an heirloom from the family collection."

"I can't just throw it away, can I?" To her surprise a half sob stuck in her throat. The depth of the emotion she felt both surprised and alarmed her—she thought she had finished dealing with that part of her life, that the past could no longer reach out and hurt her.

She struggled for control. "I suppose it's only natural to remember your first engagement when you're about to become officially engaged again," she confessed. "I guess I've been wondering if it was something I did, or didn't do, that made him leave. I wouldn't want to do it again." The attempt at humor fell flat.

She played with the ring until it came free and put it in the glove compartment of the car. "He gave that to me the night of the Haitian carnival . . . bought it at one of the booths. We were both dressed in costume, everyone was, like tonight. It was a Mardi Gras kind of feeling. He was a pirate and I—" her voice cracked, "I was so desperately in love with him I wanted to believe it was an engagement ring that he gave me."

Her father made a disparaging sound. "You always had to learn things the hard way. Not every man is honorable and selfless like Stavros. Some, like Rathe Drummond, think only of what's best for them. I know it didn't seem like it at the time, but things worked out for the best for you, in the long run, didn't they?"

Unsure now of her feelings, she didn't answer him.

The pain of her first love should have ceased long ago. She wasn't one to dwell on past mistakes and had tried to put all memory of this one from her mind. Only lately those memories had come back to haunt her.

"Do you suppose I'll ever feel for Stavros what I once felt for Rathe?" It was the first time she had spoken his name aloud in years and the question was put more to herself than to her father.

He answered her anyway, the faintly disturbed quality returning to his voice the way it always had whenever he was forced to remember the man. "I don't know, but I'll tell you this—sometimes I think we might all be better off if we put our trust and faith and love in someone who is stable and steady, like Stavros, who values what is right for you more than anything else. I can tell you that he will love you in a way Rathe Drummond never could have."

"I know that." She looked at his profile curiously. "It bothers you to talk about this doesn't it?" The subject of her first love was one they both preferred to forget.

"No," he said. "It doesn't bother me to talk about it if it helps you."

She felt that her father's reply was more considerate of her feelings than honest. She mused, "He was a special man in my life; I just can't pretend he never existed." Her expression grew soft in memory. "He was so vitally alive that it made me feel excited just being in the same room with him. I remember when I first met him; you recall, it was in your study when he was trying to convince you to finance his salvage expedition with all the boats and equipment...."

"And what decided me in the end was your offering him the use of your boat and your guide services... for free, all summer. I had to send extra men and equipment then, just to keep an eye on you," he grumbled. "Not that it did any good. You were an impulsive, headstrong little girl even then. You haven't changed much."

She grinned at him fondly, quite sure that twenty years

from now he would still refer to her as a little girl. "I was eighteen, hardly a little girl," she reminded him. "I know you didn't approve of how serious we were about our relationship. I was so sure we would get married when the summer was over, after he'd finished the job, especially after he bought me the ring. I thought he loved me."

"But he didn't." Her father's harsh words brought her back to earth. "And I don't think you really did either, or you wouldn't have told him he was nothing to you but a summer romance, that he could never be suitable on a permanent basis for you."

She was surprised that he remembered her quote verbatim. "I had to save my pride; it was all I had left after I heard him tell you he had no intention of giving me the kind of marriage and security you demanded. I would have been humiliated if he had realized my true feelings, so I lied."

He pulled into the parking lot across the street from the marina club's entrance and stopped the engine. "What are your true feelings now? This is a big step you're planning, this announcement of your engagement to Stavros tonight, formally. I want it for you, but I do want you to be happy. That has always been my goal."

She closed her eyes to the distractions outside and turned her thoughts within. "Do you know that for years after he left me I hoped he would come back? When he didn't, I was hurt, very hurt. I vowed that I would never love so blindly again. I've kept that promise to myself. I've never loved that way again. What I feel for Stavros is more like the glowing coals of a fire than a raging inferno. I know he's always going to be there for me. I feel secure with him, and safe." She opened her eyes to look at him and winked, comforting him with her smile. "Is that what you wanted to hear?"

"That's what I wanted to hear."

She pinned a curl back absentmindedly. The veiled, uncertain look had gone from her face. Her moment of decision had come, and there was no reason for her to look back at the past. Before the night was over she would be engaged, officially, to marry Stavros Halkias.

Her father ushered her out of the car and to the marina club's entrance. The highly polished floor resounded with the sound of their footsteps as they approached the room in which the party was being held. The sound of tinkling glasses and muted conversation grew appreciatively louder as her father held the inner doors open, allowing her to enter first. The walls were a colorful collage of various pirate flags, Spanish lace, daggers, and anchor chain; the backdrop for the bandstand was a picture of *Mutiny on the Bounty*. There were chests spilling over with "loot"—painted gold coils and costume jewelry. Weathered barrels of rum threatened to topple the bar on which they stood alongside huge copper tubs filled with ice and bottles of champagne. And the dance floor abounded with able-bodied seamen and first mates. A slew of captains in their white, powdered wigs and fancy silk hose escorted fine English ladies, and buccaneers consorted with underdressed bawdy streetwalkers. It was 1717 on New Providence Island, and Nassau was filled tonight with booty-laden frigates and the smell of spice and seawater.

As Lorelei entered on her father's arm, a hush settled over the gathering, and friends and others she knew through her business came forward to greet her. The small company that had gathered around her parted, however, as a blond buccaneer moved through their ranks.

"Your father said your costume had to be seen to be believed, and I totally agree." A low whistle alerted her to Stavros, dressed as a pirate. She closed her mind to another pirate who intruded once again on her thoughts. "I was afraid you had decided not to come," he continued, "but I can see you must have spent all this time and effort making yourself beautiful."

She flirted with him in mock affront. "Are you saying sir, that it takes extra time and effort to make me beautiful?"

In answer, he swung her out onto the dance floor and into a romantic dip, straight out of an old movie. "My lovely siren, were it not for the fact that my mother is watching us at this very moment I would show you with more than words just how beautiful I think you are, even without your elaborate costume." Humorous glints flashed in her eyes and the heavily accented voice sounded vaguely akin to Charles Bronson's. In fact, it was so unlike Stavros's usual light tones that she had to laugh, and struggled to regain her balance.

"Stop it!" she commanded. "And I thought *I* was going to be the one to make a spectacle of us."

"Unhand that woman at once, young man!" The great, swaggering bulk of Stavros's father stood squarely in front of them, his bearded face set in pretended severity. In the spirit of things, he was dressed as an English king; and in purple velvet and fur, his corpulent figure could easily have been that of King Henry VIII, if that royal man had been Greek.

"I've come to take Lorelei for a dance before my wife takes her off to meet some society person or another and deprives me of my rights as the future father-in-law of the bride."

She smiled gaily and waved Stavros away, letting his father guide her in the graceful, sedate steps of a waltz, ignoring the fact that their dance neither matched the pace of the music nor followed the girations of anyone else on the floor. His huge hand held hers in a dignified manner, never holding her any closer than propriety allowed— obviously this was the man who had taught Stavros his Old World manners.

"You don't mind if I take you away from all the excitment for a few moments, do you child?" He nodded to the young couples who twirled and swirled around them.

"No, I should say not. I'd rather dance with you anyway, Papa Halkias." She had called him papa, as Stavros did, long before there was even a hint of romance, because the familiar endearment suited him.

"Why is that, my child? Because I do not protest when you trip over my feet, or because I am big enough to catch your fall when you do?" His laugh was deep and rumbling, and caused a few heads to turn in their direction. She blushed prettily, confessing the truth.

"You know I'm not used to these things." She held up one slim ankle, perched atop a very high, spiked heel.

"All this fuss—" Papa Halkias waved his hand in the air gesturing around the room, "—is not pushing you too fast, is it, child? In Greece, many times, our young girls do not even see their husbands before the ceremony, and if they find companionship and friendship afterward—" he shrugged philosophically, "—then, so much the better. It is good enough. My own marriage was just such a one. But you American girls are so much more free. Not that it is bad . . . never think so," he hastened to reassure her. "Our girls are married at a very young age, before they are even aware of men. Their husbands are all they know, and they are satisfied. But, because of your customs, you have had the opportunity to date other men, and I sometimes wonder if you have found the love you were brought up to expect. I only want you to be happy, my child, and I want you to be sure, for I have grown to love you like a daughter."

The dinner gong sounded opportunely at that moment, saving her from answering. She didn't think she could have lied to Papa Halkias, and what could she have said to reassure him when he had only echoed her own fears?

Stavros and her father joined them then and the ticklish subject was dropped and forgotten as they hurried to find an uncrowded dining spot. Great oak captain's tables had been set up in the adjoining hall. The dim electric lighting from lamps that once burned whale oil illuminated the canvas sails adorning the walls but hid the identity of the steaming concoctions in large pewter bowls already placed on the tables. Lorelei sniffed and concentrated hard, trying to identify the unusual smells wafting up from the serving dishes.

"What is it?" She peered closer but the food remained a mystery, unidentifiable until Stavros handed her a hand-printed menu. "Salmagundi..." She read aloud for the benefit of the other diners. "A traditional genuine pirate's fare, served on New Providence Island during the 1700s, containing fish, pork, chicken, corned beef, ham, duck, and sometimes turtle that has been chopped, marinated, and cooked in spiced wine and mixed with olives, grapes, mangoes, hard-boiled eggs—" she raised her eyes heavenward in a gesture of mock dismay and continued, "—onions, and a splash of oil and vinegar." Though the traditional dish sounded far from appetizing, Lorelei refused to put a damper on her celebration and quickly partook of the mixture. Following her lead, all the guests tasted the mess, tentatively at first, then with more gusto, as the salmagundi proved to be more palatable than it had either looked or sounded.

Pleased at her brave behavior, Stavros wiped his mouth on a fine linen napkin and, putting his arm about her shoulders, poured her another glass of the bubbling champagne. "Salmagundi was traditionally served with rum, so maybe that is why you don't like it."

"But I *do* like it," she countered, "now that I've tasted it; and if anything, the champagne makes it better. But it's so unusual."

"The champagne? Unusual?" He smiled teasingly and inched closer to her. "Only if you are used to drinking poor-quality beer."

"Are you making a social comment about me? You wretch!" she scolded and laughed softly. "You know that's not what I meant."

"I know. I just like to see you angry; your eyes sparkle as much as your dress. What is it made of ... cobwebs?"

The champagne and the warmth of the building had gone to her head, making her seduction almost a pleasant thing. For seduction it was, though she knew Stavros would not try to go beyond set limits this night. He was too well controlled for that, and had never done more than kiss her lips lightly. His fingers found the nape of her neck, winding themselves around the soft curls there, and he touched the transparent material of her bodice, lifting the edges slightly to allow his fingertips to caress the smoothness of her skin just underneath in a circular, rhythmic motion.

"You can sing for me anytime, my siren, and gladly will I crash my ship against your shores." His voice was like the soft feel of velvet on her ear.

The intimate moment passed swiftly, and Lorelei wanted to linger in its delicious mood, when she suddenly realized that something was different. Silence, complete silence, now ruled the once-noisy ballroom. But before she could question it, it was broken by the sound of a drumroll. Mama Halkias, her whole vibrant being made twice as alive by excitement, gestured to the bandleader's microphone.

"Lorelei, Stavros," she whispered, "now's the time to announce your engagement."

Papa Halkias looked at her reproachfully, but the hint of a smile played on his lips. "I think your timing could have been better, Helene."

"It's all right, mama, we're ready." Stavros was already on his feet and bringing her with him, though for some unaccountable reason her heart was beating very fast and a cold sweat had dampened her clinging costume, robbing her of her strength. The band and the audience were silent as Stavros placed a brilliant diamond engagement ring on her finger.

CHAPTER TWO

LORELEI WAS TREMBLING, feeling horribly guilty at her unspoken deception. Stavros obviously expected a commitment that she now suspected she couldn't give. How could she promise her complete love and undying devotion when she had given all the love and devotion she possessed to her once-beloved pirate? Demanding, virile, Rathe Drummond had seen into her soul with his slate gray eyes and claimed it for his own. Did she have anything left in her to give Stavros?

Suddenly she blinked, startled into awareness by something she could not swear was reality or specter. Her breath was taken away and she closed her eyes for a moment and blinked again, her pupils growing into large black pools, enveloping the surrounding green. The "specter" remained, as solid as the doorway in which he stood, the gray eyes she had just remembered so vividly staring across the room at her with a ferocious intensity. "Honey, are your ready?" Stavros softly inquired, but she couldn't answer. She just gripped his hand for support, the only response she could make.

Could she stop the announcement now? Could she willfully destroy their happiness because the man who had deserted her six years ago now stared at her as though he felt an anger and a pain so intense that he could not control it? She only vaguely heard the words and the applause as the announcement was made, her eyes riveted to the man whose expression had gone blank.

The guests began to sit down or head for the dance floor, their attention thankfully short, diverted to whatever they had been doing before the announcement was made.

"Stavros . . ." she spoke haltingly. "I'm terribly warm. Would you mind very much if I stepped out onto the balcony for a breath of fresh air?"

He half rose, the satisfied smile still in place. "Do you want company?" Clearly he expected no opposition.

"No!" She couldn't help herself as the word tumbled out of its own accord. "I mean no, thank you. I won't be very long, just a breath of air." She fled the still-crowded dining room, making her way to the balcony alone. Once there she forced her mind to go entirely blank and purposefully slowed her breathing back to normal, though her hands still trembled.

From the quiet, vacant balcony, she could see the ocean, all but devoid at this time of night of boats or people. The docks were farther down and she turned away from that direction, watching, mesmerized for a few moments by the pounding of the surf. The sea always managed to calm her, the sounds of the waves crashing onto the shore comforting her whenever life's pressures seemed overwhelming.

Six long years ago she had lain awake and listened to the waves. The tide had come in on a Haitian shore, but the sound was the same, blending in with the sound of her own breathing and the feel of Rathe's heartbeat as he slept, her breast a pillow for his dark, curly head. She remembered tracing a line from his bushy eyebrows with her fingers, around the square, rugged jaw to finally touch the cleft in his chin, the sensual mouth, relaxed as he slept. The lean, whipcord hardness of his body had lain half over hers, their legs tangled together out of a desire to remain close, even in sleep. She had been careful not to awaken him. It was as if some inner voice had urged her to store up as many memories as she could, before he was gone . . .

But he wasn't gone! He was here, and he had returned after six years of silence, on the night of her engagement to another man.

"No!" The word formed on her lips, the disbelief, the denial apparent from her contorted facial features, but she couldn't make a sound or look away from the man whose presence now filled the entrance to the balcony. She retreated farther out onto the terrace, half-attempting to blend in with the decorative foliage.

"Hello, Lorelei." His voice was the same, as she had known it would be. Still, it was a moment or two before she could comprehend that he had navigated the crowded room so quickly and was now facing her as she leaned against the railing. It was as if the six years had never passed; he looked no older and had changed very little. His six-foot three-inch frame had been out in the sun and his muscles were a bit more developed, the tan three-piece suit molding itself to him well, emphasizing his lean thighs and all-over athletic physique. His mouth was firmer, his jawline less yielding. All these changes only served to make him even more ruggedly handsome than she remembered. But it was his eyes that bothered her the most; a deep gray green, they were the color of the sea on a stormy night and every bit as cold.

"What are you doing here?" she asked. Like a hypnotized bird before the snake, she watched him, unable to move from the spot she seemed to be rooted to. "What do you want? This is a private, by-invitation-only party, and I'm quite sure you don't have one . . . an invitation, I mean."

Unlike Stavros's voice, Rathe's was naturally deep and husky and as he spoke it carried undertones of suppressed anger. "No, Lorelei, I do not have an invitation, but I had to come. Nassau is full of rumors about you and Halkias and I wanted to know if they were true. I see that they are. I came to offer my . . . congratulations."

"You've given them, so you can go," she said quickly. Her green eyes flashed with wariness and fear—fear of the effect he still had on her. "There's no reason for you to stay."

He plucked a handful of leaves from one of the expensive decorative plants and dropped them slowly, one by one, over the edge of the balcony, watching their descent with apparent interest. "I see you've changed," he said, and there was no mistaking the cynicism in his tone. "Halkias and his family must be pleased that the tomboy has transformed herself into a lady. New hairstyle, new clothes, expensive jewelry, expensive tastes all around. Very cosmopolitan, very chic. You'll look right at home in their glass display case."

Shocked by his words, she responded to him angrily. "I have no intention of standing here all evening while you make ridiculous remarks. I'm going back to my fiancé. Now, will you leave, or shall I call security to come for you?" He turned his attention from the view to her, giving the impression of a half-tamed wild animal, ready to spring on unwary prey. She was a little frightened.

"And what will you tell them, my pretty siren, that one of your lovers who wanted to see you just one . . . last . . . time refuses to leave? That would go over big with your future mama-in-law."

Lorelei bit her lower lip to keep from screaming. There had been a time when she would have given her soul to hear him say that he wanted to see her again. But why had he come back now? Now, when she had begun to believe in some sort of happiness without him? He could not hope to step back into her life where he had left off. Her fear must have communicated itself to him because he sneered derisively.

"No, I don't want you for myself. It would take more than that silly outfit to entice me anywhere near you again." He took a step closer, belying his words. "I wanted to look at you, objectively this time, to see if there is anything about you to warn a man about the kind of woman you are under that tempting surface." He studied her intently. "You're all fire and ice, aren't you? I wonder if I shouldn't warn that poor devil in there about what he's letting himself in for, that you'll wait until he's head over heels in love with you before you leave him. He seems nice enough and he surely doesn't deserve that kind of hell, the kind of hell I went through. Lord, I shouldn't have come." He ran a large, calloused hand through his thick hair and closed his eyes to the sight of her standing before him.

"No, you shouldn't have come." She repeated his admission with greater conviction. "I have every intention of marrying Stavros and I *don't* plan to leave him."

"No, I don't suppose you do. He's bought and paid for you, hasn't he? He's met your father's price; he's promised you a way of life that I wouldn't give you." She forced herself to keep even the slightest flicker of emotion from crossing her face. "I have to give you credit. You play the game well. Your love life for the past six years has been above reproach, and your expression doesn't give away your feelings. No one would guess that you don't really love him; no one would guess that hidden inside that beautiful, polished exterior is a woman who made love to a man she wasn't married to, on an open beach on Haiti, with the waves washing over their bodies, the moonlight shining on their skin..."

"Stop it! Stop it!" she cried. "I don't want to remember that."

He jerked her to his chest, crushing her against him. His hands ran over her back and hips possessively.

"Well, I remember, Lorelei. Too many nights I've remembered." His face was within inches of hers, his look intense, explosive. "Damn you, you *are* a siren..."

The things he said made no sense. *He* was the one who had left her so long ago; she was the one with a right to feel bitter, to feel lonely at night, to feel haunted by her memories, but she didn't have time to react to his words. The kiss that followed them was bitter, even brutal, leaving her lips bruised and faintly tinged with blood as he ground his mouth over hers, as if he were trying to punish her for something. It was cruel and cold, yet from somewhere within her she felt the unquestionable beginnings of desire. How dare he make her feel this way. How dare he insult her on one hand and humiliate her by forcing her to respond to him on the other. She blocked the tumultuous emotions that were filling her body and went wooden in his arms. She could not allow him to see how deeply he still affected her, would not give him that satisfaction again.

Suddenly he held her away from him. "My God, I am almost sorry for Halkias. He's paying a high price for a beautiful, lifeless doll, an ice maiden, and not even a virgin one at that. I wonder if he knows . . . knows what you really are, Lorelei?" His voice was harsh and resounded hollowly in her ears. She almost doubled over in pain, and the eyes so full of anger just an instant before suddenly became full of concern. "What kind of game are you playing now?"

The wrought-iron railing was cold and solid under her fingers, and she grasped it desperately before putting her hands to her face and allowing the blackness of the night to invade her senses. She felt the firm hands once again, around her body, oddly gentle this time, then the coldness of the balcony's marble bench as the hands were removed. Curiously bereft, she would have reached out for them again if another voice had not intruded.

"Lorelei? Sweetheart, are you okay? Did you fall? Are you hurt?" The questions ran together as Stavros spoke. "I should never have let her come out here alone."

"She will be fine, Stavros." Papa Halkias moved his son aside and pressed a cool cloth to her forehead, his voice as soothing as his hands. "Our little mermaid has only been standing on her pretty new legs too long today. She is not used to champagne, or to all the excitement, and I fear the salmagundi is enough to make anyone feel faint, is it not, child?"

He questioned her gently, but she felt disheveled and

cheapened somehow after her encounter with Rathe. It
was an effort to appear normal. She managed to get to
her feet but was too shaken to walk.

"You must take her home now, Stavros. She should
be in bed. There will be time enough later to be together."
He dropped a light kiss on her forehead and cleared a
path for them to the car.

She sent up a silent prayer in thanks; Helene Halkias
was occupied elsewhere, and just as luckily her father
had gone home early, leaving the couple alone. She
sighed in relief and sank down into the passenger's seat,
and waited for Stavros to let himself in on the opposite
side. She was still pale and shaky and she knew she
couldn't hide her state. Papa Halkias was too much of
a gentleman to question what had taken place on the
balcony, even if he had seen Rathe's departure. And, as
Rathe had so contemptuously insinuated earlier, neither
Stavros nor Papa Halkias knew anything about her relationship with him, so there was no reason for either of
them to question her; and in any case, Stavros never
pushed, never pried, never questioned her about anything, though if anyone had a right to do so, it was he.
Her father was another matter, and she breathed a sigh
of relief that he was gone. He would never sit in silence
wondering what had taken place. Even if he had not seen
Rathe, he would see the changes in her and demand to
know what was wrong. But Stavros was different, more
worried about how she felt than why she felt that way,
and his concern made her feel guilty and grateful at the
same time.

"Feeling better now, sweetheart?" The car stopped in
front of her house and Stavros turned off the engine,
apparently content to wait until she was sure of an answer. The sea and the softly singing crickets relaxed her
a little, as did the concealing cloak of darkness.

"Yes, I think I do, and I want to apologize for taking
you away from the party."

He grinned. "Do you mean to tell me this wasn't a

clever ruse to get me out here alone, away from all those
prying eyes? Well, my dear, I refuse to let you off scot-
free." His teasing laughter stopped as he sought her lips,
seeking, his tongue exploring the softness of her inner
mouth, still tender from Rathe's brutal assault. She returned his kiss, reveling in its undemanding warmth, the
gentleness of his love. Here was a man she could understand, who was open and honest, with no hidden
bitterness, no mysterious animosity or pain.

She could feel his hands shake as they touched the
semitransparent material of her dress, his fingers barely
a caress as they brushed over her thinly veiled breasts,
his hands cupping their soft roundness for only an instant
before he pushed her gently from him, taking her face
in his hands instead, tilting it so that he could read the
expression there.

"You had really better go in now," he said softly.

"But why?" She was not used to thinking of him as
a lover, but she was not adverse to the few tentative
advances he had made so far.

"Anyone would think you straight out of a convent
to ask me that question. Let's just say that I don't want
to take advantage of your trust at this stage of the game."

She lowered her eyes and played with the buttons on
his shirt. "We *are* going to be married you know," she
teased him lightly. "And I'm sure you'd do the honorable
thing by me. I trust you, Stavros, and I'm not afraid of
you," she whispered.

"Maybe I'm afraid of you." He covered her fingers
with his, preventing her from touching the smooth skin
of his chest. "I'll give you an hour to stop that—or else,
Lorelei."

His sense of humor had not gotten lost in all the
excitement after all. Her heart swelled with tenderness
for him. If only she could feel as strongly for him physically as she did emotionally, if only he aroused her in
the same way that Rathe . . . she banished that traitorous
thought from her mind.

"Nope." She smiled impishly and allowed her hands to finish the job of unbuttoning his shirt. The material was satiny soft, as was his chest, and she lay her head against him in contentment.

"Lorelei, do you want me to make love to you?"

It was a sincere question that she wished she had the answer to. She did want him to, in a way, but not for the reasons he would believe. She *had* to know if she could feel passion for him. She had closed off those feelings for so long, perhaps she was incapable of them.

"I . . . I don't know." She shook her head in consternation. It was a terrible admission to make to the man one had just become engaged to marry. For the second time in one evening she felt the burning sting of tears. What was happening to her calm poise? Had she fought to regain it at eighteen years of age only to lose it at a mature twenty-five? And what of Stavros? She looked up at him, expecting to see anger or hurt, even embarrassment, but she was unprepared for his jovial grin.

"Crazy girl—is that what's bothering you? Look, I don't expect you to feel passion for me now, with your limited experience." He kissed the tip of her nose. "When the time comes, I will be the one to teach you all you need to know about love. You won't have to do the chasing and there won't be any doubts for you then. But for now, be just a little Greek, eh? Be happy that we are friends. You will grow to feel more; you have my promise. But for now, you must go inside if you want to wear white on our wedding day, or I might be tempted to give you lessons in love early, in this not so very comfortable front seat of my car."

Lorelei bit her lip in indecision. When the unfortunate summer with Rathe was over, she had been too humiliated and ashamed to admit her short-lived affair to anyone, and in any case, she had no close girlfriends in whom to confide. Later, it never occurred to her to share her past with anyone, least of all her conservative Greek friend with his traditional outlook on everything, including premarital sex. Her experience with Rathe had been her private mistake, a painful part of her past that she preferred to forget. There had been no serious dating before Stavros, and none after, and so he could be forgiven for thinking her an innocent; but now, she could think of no suitable way to correct his assumption.

Troubled, she kissed him a preoccupied good night and made her way into the house alone, and in darkness. She couldn't risk waking her father, not tonight. She was too bone weary both physically and emotionally for another confrontation. The matter of Rathe Drummond, and how she could avoid him in the future, would have to wait until morning.

She skipped the hot shower she had been contemplating and, throwing her costume off, tumbled into bed. She fell asleep almost before her head touched the pillow, her hand unconsciously clenched around the diamond engagement ring lest the happiness that it promised be snatched away from her at the last moment. She was officially engaged to be married to Stavros Halkias, and there wasn't room in her soon-to-be-structured life for a long-ago Mardi Gras pirate who once taught her the joys of what it meant to be a woman.

CHAPTER THREE

LORELEI STRETCHED AND yawned and snuggled farther down into the warm bed again, covering her tangled hair with a pillow. It was early; it had to be, although she hadn't glanced up at the clock to make sure, hadn't, as a matter of fact, opened her eyes. But it was quiet outside, and it was never quiet in her neighborhood except in the very early morning. Yet something had disturbed her slumber and she forced herself to remain awake, straining to hear if whatever it was would come again.

She sat up then, recognizing the dull tapping against the windowpane as the "something" that had roused her originally. She rubbed her eyes sleepily, drew on a scarlet nylon robe, and swung her feet to the floor to investigate, sucking in her breath as her feet touched the cool damp surface of the bare wood floor. She pulled the curtains back.

"Stavros?" The window latch was stuck and she tugged at it for a few seconds before it came free. "Stavros, what on earth are you doing down there?" Her voice was husky with sleep and her eyes weren't fully open, but she was aware of Stavros's condition anyway.

Her usually immaculate fiancé was still dressed in last night's costume. Out of place now, smudged here and there and rumpled, it smelled of smoke and the heady aroma of whiskey. His pale eyes were bloodshot and tired, as if he had been up all night. But his speech was clear, excited even, so the binge, if that's what it had been, must have been less drastic than his looks led her to believe.

"I'm sorry, but I need to talk to you. I thought you'd never wake up."

"Well, I can't let you in through my bedroom window. Give me a minute and I'll open the front door." But she had forgotten to lock the front entrance last night, and he was already inside before she could get there, eagerly pulling her along to the privacy of the kitchen before he spoke.

"I have the greatest idea—that is, I've been offered the best proposition. It involves the two of us and I thought—"

She put a finger to his lips, effectively silencing the excited monologue.

"You might be wide awake—" she poked him gingerly in the chest, "—but I'm not, so give me a minute."

She yawned widely and measured coffee and water, managing to get each into its rightful place and plug in the coffee maker before pulling the pale blue kitchen curtains aside to admit the watery, pre-morning sunlight.

"It's not morning yet, Stavros. What are you doing?"

His voice was raised in excitement, but before he could say one complete word she interrupted. "Hush! I don't want to wake up dad before dawn." She sat down at the table beside him. "Now, what did you do, have an early bachelor party?" She surveyed his crumpled attire.

He held his head ruefully. "Mmmmm... not really, though I think my head would disagree with me this morning. I went back to the party after I dropped you off and I met someone." He chuckled regretfully. "Come to think of it, maybe I did overindulge; for the life of me, I can't remember his name."

Her delicately arched eyebrows lifted skeptically. "You're sure it was a *him* and not a *her?*"

"It was a man. The only woman I wanted last night was you." A frown of concentration turned the corners of his mouth down, and he sipped the coffee she poured without being aware that he did so, then shrugged. "Oh well, it will come to me later, I guess. Anyway, that's not the important part. What is important is that he has found a seventeeeth-century Spanish galleon, or what's left of it, here in the Bahamas, and he needs a small crew to help salvage it. He needs divers, and he wants me."

Tired as he obviously was, his whole being was filled with excitement. She had never seen him so animated. Sitting on the edge of his chair, he looked about to take flight, his arms moving this way and that.

"From what he tells me has already been brought up, it's a quality find, with a capital Q. It's just a miracle someone hasn't discovered it before now. As it is, only he and the two other divers he's hired know exactly where the ship is."

He raised four fingers. "Besides the divers, he needs a photographer—I think he has already hired someone for that job—and someone to help him catalogue and identify the artifacts brought up. But that's all."

"Small operation," she commented, though she could not help reflecting that the man who'd found this galleon sounded typical of someone Stavros's parents would know—wealthy, most likely, and able to indulge each of his interests until it was supplanted by the next.

"He's very worried about security. He thinks the fewer people on the crew, the better, and he did stress that anyone who comes to work for him has to sign a contract promising to spend the three months he thinks are required to salvage the ship in seclusion, with no contact from the outside."

She laughed. "What melodrama. Where is this place, the moon?"

"I can't say." He hedged. "I promised not to."

She was astonished. "I don't know, isn't that kind of tight? You'd think he was James Bond and it was a secret mission or something. If it is here, as you say, in the

Bahamas, he won't succeed in keeping it a secret forever."

He nodded. "True, but he won't have to keep it a secret forever. It's just that, aside from the economic repercussions that would result if word gets out about how fantastic this find is, there is the problem of these so-called pirates. With the amount of money involved, he really needs armed guards and barbed wire; but in the first place, it isn't practical for the location, and in the second, the guards themselves would attract attention to the site. He can't afford the publicity."

"I suppose I can understand that," she agreed. "I didn't realize at first how big this was, but does he really expect his crew to have no contact with anyone at all for how long . . . three months? No one is going to go for that."

Some of the exuberance left his face. "He expects it from the crew he has hired. He expects it from me. I signed the contract last night." Then, seeing the stunned expression on her face, he said, "Please don't be angry with me. This is the chance I have been waiting for."

He took her hands earnestly, making her ashamed of the envious thoughts that filled her mind. He was leaving on what seemed to be a wonderful job, and she was staying here. She sighed. "Oh, Stavros, how could I be angry?" She hugged him affectionately. I am happy for you, truly I am. It's just that I'll miss you. We haven't had too much time together for the past few weeks, and your mother will be wanting to set the wedding date. I would hate to be married on the day you get back from . . . wherever this place is."

"Sweetheart, I know that. I want to be with you as well and that's why I want to take you with me."

"Stavros, if your employer . . . whose name you can't remember . . . is such a stickler for security, he's not going to allow his employees to bring their friends or fiancées."

Stavros's expression remained hopeful. "That's right. In fact, no one is allowed on site, unless they are working for him. He had a lucky break when he hired two divers in the same family. The father and the son dive, and the mother and daughter do something else for him... housekeeping... bookkeeping, I think. I'm not sure. Anyway, he's having a very hard time finding someone to catalogue his finds."

"I can see why."

Stavros shrugged. "He pays well."

"You can't buy loyalty. You either trust your people or you don't," she declared.

"Well, be that as it may, the professionals aren't willing to leave their other work and their families behind for such a long time, and he won't hire them any other way. So, I told him I knew of someone who was experienced and might be willing to come right away and live with his restrictions."

"Who?" She mentally ran over the list of their mutual friends, unable to think of any who would fit his description.

"You," he replied. "You would be perfect for the job—far above anyone else he's going to get to come, considering his conditions, and I feel sure you could do the work. Just think of it—three months on a virtually deserted island without one member of my family ... almost alone... just the two of us."

"The site is near the island?"

"Yes."

She gave him a pained look. "I have done quite a bit of diving from the boat, and I have found a few wrecks, though nothing so old as the seventeeth century. I've studied the history of the Bahamas and I know how to identify most of what could be found down there; but, Stavros, I don't have any professional credentials and you can't say that I'm experienced."

"Think about it, please," he urged her.

She considered the proposal. It certainly would be heavenly to have a change of scene; she'd thought that just a few minutes ago. And it would be nice to have Stavros all to herself for a while before the wedding, to

take the time to see him in a more romantic setting. Their
schedules were so different now, and she worked such
erratic hours, that if she didn't go with him, it could be
like marrying a stranger when he returned. But even for
that, she couldn't lie about her qualifications.

"Do you want some breakfast?" she asked him, stall-
ing for time. She could never concentrate on an empty
stomach and, busying herself at the stove, she cracked
eggs into a buttered pan and popped bread into the toaster
without his confirmation.

That was another nice thing about Stavros, another
point in his favor: he ate her cooking without complaint,
though she was well aware that he refrained from asking
her anything while she was in the process. She used that
fact to her advantage this morning. Cooking required her
utmost concentration, and he didn't speak a work until
she had set his breakfast and hers on the table before
them. He took a bite, nodded his approval, then set the
fork aside for the time being.

"I know what you're thinking. You're thinking that
you couldn't possibly accept because you aren't that qualified. But you would actually be doing the man a favor
if you would accept. He as much as told me last night
that if he didn't find someone immediately, he would
have to do the work himself, and that would slow down
the entire operation, as he's normally a diver, like me."

She drummed her fingers on the table, wanting to be
convinced, but not as yet persuaded.

"And when I told him I could come up with somebody,
he said he would be very grateful. I know he has to pick
up supplies, do some other errands, and be back on site
tomorrow, so he won't have time to do any looking."

She responded in exasperation. "So what am I supposed to do? Even if I could just quit the tour business
for three months, you said yourself that he was leaving
tomorrow for—you won't tell me where—and you
say you can't remember his name. So how am I supposed
to apply?"

Stavros looked sly and scooped up some egg with a piece of toast. "I brought the contract over with me. He gave it to me last night and said that if I could get anyone qualifed to sign on the dotted line, I was to bring him with me."

"*Him?*" she repeated.

"Or her. It doesn't matter. There are other woman on the site."

She wanted to believe him. There'd be no problem in leasing her boat out for three or four months, especially since it was now the height of the season. It would also be fascinating to see things untouched by human hands for over three hundred years, if the wreck really was that old. Even more important, what chance would she have of running into Rathe Drummond where she was going? None, she assured herself with a satisfied smile. The more she thought about the idea, the more it appealed to her.

"Well," he demanded. "What do you think?"

Her face was a mask of casual indifference, and she shrugged her shoulders eloquently.

"I . . . don't . . . know," she drawled slowly, giving the impression that she was not all that interested.

"Lorelei, don't tease me," he begged. "You are coming with me. If I hadn't have been sure that you would . . ." He looked pitiful.

"That should teach you to take me for granted." She backed away from him, a mischievous gleam in her green eyes.

"Don't say that, Lorelei, say yes," he pleaded with her.

"No." She laughed, tossing back her head, making the gleaming dark hair cascade further down her back.

"Yes, even if I have to carry you and drag you off." She shrieked as he threw her up and over his shoulder, moaning all the while he did so.

"Uggh! I hope you won't be sadistic enough to make me carry you all the way."

She pounded on his back. "Put me down, muscles. I don't see how you expect to bring up these loads of treasure if you can't lift a skinny-bones like me. I guess I'll just have to go along to give you a hand."

"Skinny? Ha!" He pinched the curved softness of her hips, then, realizing what she had said, gave a whoop of joy. "You mean you'll come?"

"If you're sure he'll have me, and if you'll *put me down!*"

He twirled her around the kitchen before letting her feet come to the floor.

"If I'm sure he'll have you? If? He would be losing the best team of the century if he doesn't. Oh, I do love you, Lorelei."

In looking back, Lorelei couldn't believe it had all happened so quickly. Once her decision to go was made, the actual signing of the contract in front of a notary public took place that morning. Her packing and the saying of good-byes, even the leasing of her tour boat to a friend, had been taken care of the next day. It was as if some unseen hand of fate had decided to push her on to her destination. The only cloud on the horizon was that fate had not seen fit to push Stavros's affairs as quickly, and though he planned to take her out to the island site that afternoon, he would have to turn right around and sail back to Nassau to settle his own business.

And when they kissed good-bye, she clung to him half-fearfully, wondering if this might be the last time she would feel so secure in his arms. The feeling startled her—why had such a strange thought entered her head?

CHAPTER FOUR

ANDROS, THE ISLAND nearest the wreck site, was almost deserted. Normally she would have been delighted at the prospect of spending time alone on it, but as she stood on the small, crescent-shaped beach and waved Stavros away, the feeling of apprehension stole over her once more. It wasn't that she was nervous exactly. She had a copy of the signed contract in the pocket of her blue sun dress, and despite her original reservations, she felt reasonably sure she could handle the work. The island itself was not the problem. It was a beautiful place with white sandy beaches and warm, fish-filled turquoise water. She couldn't put a finger on whatever it was that made her want to go back to Nassau. Perhaps the loneliness... she shook off the feeling and concentrated on her surroundings, absorbing the island's loveliness.

The rickety wooden pier was empty now that the sound of Stavros's boat had died away, and only the sound of the wind, as it whispered through the coconut palms, remained. The beach was entirely deserted, unless she counted the sand crab that hastily scuttled away, resentful of her presence, or the population of hungry seagulls that squalled angrily overhead. Only that pier and a vine-covered path gave any indication that man had ever set foot on this particular piece of paradise.

She lugged her bags toward the path, thankful that she could make do with the minimum of clothes as her feet sank deeply into the sand. With difficulty she wound her way through the undergrowth, following the faint outline of a geometric structure that could be seen through the trees.

"At least the directions were right." She huffed and puffed her way through the deep sand and parted the last of the wild bougainvillea that climbed on anything and everything sturdy enough to hold its weight. She gasped in awe at the building ahead.

"I'm lost. This can't be it," she said to herself. There had been no description of the site buildings, other than that there were supposed to be rooms for the team to stay in while working, but there had never been a mention of the colossal building ahead of her! It could once have been an elegant plantation mansion. Two-storied, its natural limestone washed a brilliant white, it stood, majestic, atop a small knoll. Six graceful columns rose from the ground floor to the roof and supported the veranda that shaded the lower floor. There was a profusion of brightly colored flowers, delicious purple and red bougainvillea, red and yellow hibiscus, growing up to the veranda. Huge picture windows on both floors looked slightly out of character and had probably been added later, but she knew they would give an excellent view of the sea, as the knoll overlooked the beach. She ascended the stone steps to the front door with some trepidation. The ornate brass door knocker resounded loudly at her touch, and though the door itself was of a very heavy oak, she could hear the faint sound of footsteps from inside.

"Hello, so you're the new diver?" The woman who opened the door seemed to be in her late forties. Short and plump, she was dressed in a fashionable mid-length dress that unfortunately did little to enhance her stocky figure. On second glance the dress gave the impression of being serviceable rather than fashionable, and had no doubt been saved from a time when below-the-knee dresses had been in style. The brassy, hennaed hair was pin-curled, and her makeup looked as though it had been put on with a heavy hand in the dark, or by a preschooler with his first set of crayons. But the dark red smear of lipstick didn't detract from her friendly smile, and a fleet of welcoming laugh lines couldn't be hidden under the pancake and rouge.

"I'm Lucy Yates," she introduced herself. "Won't you come in?" A work-reddened hand was thrust at her and Lorelei took it, finding herself being pulled into the cool recesses of the large house.

"Actually, I'm not the diver," Lorelei explained. "He dropped me off here, but he had to return to Nassau to clear up a few things. He'll be back in a day or so. I've been hired to do the cataloguing. My name is Lorelei Averill."

Lucy looked uncertain. "The boss didn't say anything."

Lorelei produced the document from the pocket of her sun dress and handed it to the woman. "From what I understand, the boss gave my fiancé—the other diver— carte blanche in choosing someone to do the job. He gave him a contract, which I signed back in Nassau, so your boss probably doesn't know I'm coming unless Stavros radioed or telephoned him."

Lucy accepted that explanation without a fuss. "I wouldn't know about any messages. The only communication here is on the boats and the boss is out there now, unloading some supplies, so if your fiancé radios he'll get the word first."

"Should I go tell him I've arrived?"

"That won't be necessary," a cold voice intoned. "I'm back."

At the sound of the voice, Lorelei froze. No, it couldn't be—she turned, and on seeing his face, she felt all color fade from her own. There had been no mistaking that deep voice now filled with sarcasm. Her new boss was none other than Rathe.

She would have given anything simply to leave the house and the island as well, but she couldn't find the courage to do so. Mercifully, Lucy didn't seem to notice that anything was wrong, and she moved to introduce them.

"Rathe," she said, "I want you to meet our new team member, Lorelei Averill."

Rathe's mouth tightened into a grim line, but his voice remained relatively emotionless. "The one Halkias promised to bring with him, I presume." He turned to Lucy. "I think I'd better speak with the new recruit alone," he informed her, keeping the tension Lorelei knew he must feel under control. "Would you excuse us for a moment?"

"Certainly," Lucy smiled. "Just call if you need me."

As soon as she was gone, Rathe exploded. "What in the name of God do you think you're doing?" he asked fiercely. "This must be some kind of practical joke, but I assure you I do not find it amusing."

"Amusing" was the last adjective she would have used, also, and her breath came out in short, nervous gasps.

"You can't think I knew you would be here when I agreed to come? The last place I would want to be is near you . . . in fact, the farther away the better."

"Then you had better explain yourself woman, and you had better make it good." He looked so angry that for a moment she was afraid, but then her own temper took over. None of this terrible nightmare had been her fault!

"Stavros didn't remember your name . . ." She paused in consternation. It was true, but very out of character for her meticulous fiancé. He was very careful to keep track of the smallest detail, and the name of the man who hired them could not be considered a small detail. It was important.

"He was excited about the contract that he hoped we'd both sign, and the only name mentioned on that is Poseidon Enterprises.

"The name of the company, of this operation." Rathe swore softly and clenched his fists, but there was no surprise in his face that Stavros had not remembered his name. "Damn the man! I thought I explained the rules to him in detail." He exploded and glared at her angrily as though he thought her responsible. "I told him this job was to be for three months . . . three months of seclusion. I thought he understood, but what does he do? He imports his girlfriend along with him." He shook his head in disbelief.

A sudden realization hit her. "You planned this, didn't you? It never entered my head until now, but you never did give Stavros your name; you purposely asked him on this assignment because you knew it would keep him away from me for at least three months! That's the most despicable thing I've ever heard of."

"But you came too." His voice was wooden.

"Yes!" She taunted him sarcastically. "And if I could stand the sight of you for three months, I'd make you pay for trying to manipulate Stavros and me. As it happens, I am qualified to tackle the job I was hired for and you couldn't get rid of me easily, if I didn't want to go. But I don't care to share this island with you, Rathe Drummond, not even to be with Stavros. In fact, I'm going to tell him all about what you tried to do, and then where will you get another diver and cataloguer who will agree to your silly contract?"

Rathe's bitter contempt convinced her that he, too, was aware of the implications.

"I see that you understand the problem. I no more wanted you here than you wanted to be here, but neither of us has much choice in the matter now. You've already threatened to blackmail me by convincing Halkias to renege on his contractual obligations. If I allow you off the island, how do I know you wouldn't blow this secret sky-high out of spite?"

"I wouldn't. You have to believe I wouldn't." She didn't care a scrap for her pride at the moment. She could not, would not, stay on Andros with Rathe.

"I know you won't, because you're not leaving this island. You've given me no sign in the past that I could count on your word, and I see no reason to make the second biggest mistake of my life by trusting you or your word again. I've worked a long, long time for this and I won't allow you to ruin my work as well as..." He stopped short, giving nothing more away.

She had no idea what he was talking about or what he would have said further, but clearly he had no intention of allowing her to leave. Urged on by a subconscious desire to escape, more than by any logical plan, she bolted, but he was by far the faster of the two and easily stopped her near the front door.

"No. Let me go!" She was fast becoming hysterical but she couldn't seem to stop herself, and she struggled in his grip as though her life depended on it.

"Will you be quiet?" Her whimper of protest was smothered as he kissed her, his mouth securely fastened onto hers as he half dragged, half carried her out the front door and onto the shaded patio.

"Have you done with the melodramatics now?" Calmed somewhat, he touched her pale face guiltily. "We're going to have to talk about this. I can't have you—"

"Who can't you have, my darling?" A deep, woman's voice inquired.

The front door to the house had opened and closed so quietly that neither Rathe nor she had time to move away from each other. The woman was not quite Rathe's height, but she towered over Lorelei's five-foot five-inch frame. She glowered at Lorelei, still within Rathe's arms. Her hair was as black as Lorelei's own, but very curly. She was sensuous, from the full, deeply rouged lips, to her more than voluptuous curves, to the dusky golden brown of her skin that looked so attractive in the fire-red dress and matching shoes. She was an amazon of a woman, and Lorelei, in her turquoise cotton sun dress, felt herself a wispy, pale thing in comparison.

"Carmen, this is Lorelei Averill. She's been signed on to do our cataloguing. Lorelei, Carmen Alvarada is our photographer."

"You didn't tell me you hired anyone on your trip to Nassau. I thought you wanted to get that historian, Dr. . . . Dr. . . . whatever his name was."

"Dr. Hargrove had other commitments, Carmen."

She mewed in regret. "So we're forced to make do with second best. I suppose she is trained though, or you would not have hired her, and she can't help but be better than the Yates girl is now." She turned her questions to Lorelei. "Did you bring your résumé? I'd like to go over it." Clearly Rathe's right-hand man, so to speak, was this woman.

"Carmen, leave it be. She doesn't have a résumé, but I'm sure she can do the work. In any case, she has already signed the contract."

"How do you know that?" she asked him in surprise. "It isn't like you to hire someone without first checking into their references, their résumé, their background. Think how thoroughly you checked me over." She smiled at him seductively.

"He didn't hire me." Lorelei interjected herself into their conversation. "My fiancé did. Rathe—Mr. Drummond—gave him a contract and told him to have someone qualified sign on the dotted line; but if you have someone else in mind, or you require extensive references, then perhaps it would be best if I went back to Nassau and allowed you to look for someone more suitable to your needs."

"No," Rathe answered her adamantly. "You signed my contract; you stay." There was a wealth of meaning behind his statement.

"Don't be so obstinate, darling. I don't think she wants to stay. It's obvious to me that her fiancé has gotten her in over her head."

The slur of her abilities was a small price to pay if she could use it to facilitate her escape. "I don't know about that, but the job isn't exactly what I was expecting, so I'm sure you're right; it would be better if I left. Would it trouble you, Miss Alvarada, to take me into Nassau tomorrow?"

"Yes, it would trouble her. She has work to do. She isn't a shuttle bus." His back was turned away from Carmen. "I don't appreciate being manipulated." He barely mouthed the threat in her direction. "Miss Averill knows too much about the project, Carmen. It would violate security if I allowed her to leave now. I'm quite sure she'll do the work. We'll just have to keep her locked up in the artifact room until she does." His eyes glittered dangerously.

"On bread and water rations, Rathe?" She pushed him further.

"Bread and water?" Lucy Yates swung the outer door open and stood in the breeze, mopping her brow with the corner of her apron. "Have you been complaining about my cooking, Rathe?" she teased. "This poor woman's just arrived, and we certainly haven't shown her any hospitality." She took Lorelei's arm. "Come with me, dear, and I'll let you taste my bread and water. You can decide for yourself." She ushered a thankful Lorelei away from the other two and into the house. Best to let Rathe believe that she was staying, she thought. It would be easier for her to get away if he didn't suspect her.

The beauty of the house temporarily took her mind off the problem confronting her. The living room that opened up to the right of the front door was huge. Its long, low-slung Mediterranean-style, dark leather couches and heavy oak end tables would have overpowered a room of ordinary proportions, but they were perfect for this grand space. Dark-chocolate-colored carpets contrasted beautifully with the whitewashed walls, and she managed to glimpse the antique grandfather clock and heavy, book-filled case before she followed Lucy through the equally elaborate dining room to the kitchen.

The kitchen looked as if it had come from the pages of a magazine, with its sparkling clean, white-enamel surfaces, the two restaurant-size refrigerators, and modern microwave oven alongside its more conventional counterpart. Only the breakfast nook, with its sunny yellow table, seemed commonplace and cozy, and it was to this spot that Lucy went, easing herself into one of the four chairs.

"Sarah, dear, my feet are awfully tired today. Could you possibly fix the young lady some tea?" She spoke to a young woman who materialized from the kitchen's large, walk-in pantry. Obviously a relation, Sarah had the same cornflower blue eyes as Lucy, the same short hair, except that the curl and color seemed natural, and her figure had not yet rounded out to plumpness.

Lucy beamed. "This is my daughter, Sarah."

The shy young girl lowered her eyes to the floor and, murmuring something unintelligible, scurried to get the tea.

Lucy lowered her voice. "My daughter's a bit shy, as you can see. We've lived on Andros all our lives and that's why I'm doubly glad you have come to work here. She needs other women closer to her age to talk to, you know."

Lorelei silently agreed that there must be only a handful of years difference between herself and the painfully shy teenager, yet she wondered how much in common she could have with the sheltered girl. Not that it really mattered; she would be gone from the island as quickly as possible. She refrained from saying anything and turned her attention to the tray of scones, jam, and tea the girl had produced before beating a hasty retreat to another part of the house.

"Ohhh, that smells heavenly." Breakfast that morning had been a hurried affair, and with the leasing of her boat, and packing, she had missed lunch altogether. And the confrontation with Rathe had drained her of whatever energy she had left.

"Made those scones myself, I did, just this morning. The butter is fresh-churned, too," she boasted proudly. "The boss likes us to be as self-sufficient as possible, and anyway, we've always looked after ourselves in that one respect, old Taylor and me. In fact, he helped me pick the strawberries for this jam last summer."

"Old Taylor?"

"My husband." Lucy took another scone and Lorelei did too.

"You are both to be congratulated, then. This is delicious."

Lucy drank her tea in short noisy slurps and brushed at a spot of jam that had slipped from the scone onto her bosom. She was a comfortable person to be around, and Lorelei regretted that she would not get to know her better.

"I'm really glad you're here," Lucy said, seemingly reading her thoughts. "Now I'll have Sarah back to help with all the cooking and cleaning."

"Do you mean the cataloguing was her job?" Lorelei managed to look stricken. "I didn't know. I understood it was vacant."

Lucy laughed reassuringly. "It would have been vacant if you hadn't come. Sarah is a born housewife. She would like nothing better than to care for a home and children, and the right man, of course. She was hoping someone else could be found to do the cataloguing, not wanting to let the boss down and all, but she was always afraid she'd drop and break something valuable, and she doesn't know the first thing about identifying what's up there." She raised her head, indicating the floor overhead. "That's more in Taylor and Ed's line, but as you said, they will be busy just bringing it all up."

"You said Taylor is your husband, but Ed is—"

"Our son." Lucy proceeded to rummage about in the pocket of her dress and pulled out a picture wallet which automatically opened up to the photograph of a thin-faced man, his short-cropped hair neither blond nor gray, but a mixture of both. Taylor, too, boasted Lucy's seemingly ever-present smile, as did the picture of the man just above him. Younger, perhaps the same age as she; the family resemblance was clear, and Lorelei was not surprised to hear this was Ed.

"Talking about me, huh?" The object of their conversation, a tall young man with sandy hair and blue eyes, sauntered into the kitchen wearing shorts and loads of beach sand. He sat and pulled the plate of scones in front of him.

"I can see why you're so tired. It's all the cooking you must have to do." Lorelei grinned at Lucy wryly.

"I can see there's no need to introduce myself, but I will anyway. The name is Ed. And you must be the new diver?" He shook her hand firmly.

"Nope." Lorelei explained again. "I guess you haven't heard either. I'm going to be trying to identify whatever you industrious divers bring up."

He whistled appreciatively. "I don't know about some of the rest of the crew, but I'm sure glad you're here. Poor Sarah was having a nervous breakdown every time we brought up a load of new stuff; besides, we could do with some pretty scenery," he teased.

"Now then, she has a fiancé, and you'll be working with him," Lucy interjected.

"Mmmm...just as well, I guess. If you are already spoken for you stand a better chance of being allowed to stay until the work is done."

Lorelei grimaced inwardly at the remark. She hated misleading these kind people.

Misinterpreting the pained look on her face, Ed hastened to reassure her. "Sorry—didn't mean to scare you. What I meant was, after you see the backlog we have up there, I hope you won't regret taking the job. Sarah was as slow as a sea turtle, and there are whole shelves that haven't even been recorded yet. And as far as not wanting you here, there's only one person who might not be agreeable. We have this nasty-tempered photographer..."

"Now hush!" Lucy commanded sharply. "Lorelei has met Carmen and I'm sure they'll get along just fine."

Ed shook his head in disagreement, and Lorelei wanted to hug him. "That she-shark? She makes it a point to attack without provocation, especially anyone who is young and female. Lorelei would have to be a super-saint to get along with her." He seemed more than willing to add to the description, but Lucy frowned disapprovingly and he changed the subject.

"How would you like to take a look-see upstairs? You might as well see what you'll be doing," he offered.

"I'd love to." Not able to bear the thought of carrying on her charade with Lucy, she felt it would be wise to leave the older woman as quickly as possible.

The staircase to the second floor was very wide and covered in the same chocolate-brown, deep-pile carpeting as the living area downstairs. Lorelei couldn't resist running her fingers along the polished smoothness of the curved banister, though it would undoubtedly leave telltale fingerprints for Lucy's dustcloth. The second story was partially open, the banister railing running down the length of hall that opened up to the many bedrooms. From what she could see as they walked by, the rooms held the same style of furniture that graced the opulent living room—antique, well-made and large, designed to draw attention and make the need for other scattered pictures, knicknacks, and accent pieces unnecessary.

"This is my room...Sarah's room...the bathroom... mom and dad's room...the other diver's room... Carmen, the she-shark's room—" he grinned wryly, sharing the joke, and waved to another room, "—the boss's room, and on the end, your room." He stopped momentarily to allow her to glance into it. It was beautiful, and her eyes were drawn from the fireplace to the bed that faced it on the opposite wall. The bedstead was of antique brass. A dusky rose bedspread and comforter matched curtains on the large picture window. The walls and carpeting were a rich ivory color harmonizing with an antique dresser, and a brass-framed mirrored dressing screen reflected the room and its furnishing beautifully.

"I must have the best room in the house," she said, silently regretting that she wouldn't be able to use it.

Then they reached the last room on the floor, which looked like it encompassed the space of several of the large rooms put together.

"You are purposely being put, madam, next to your work, so that if you should decide to burn the midnight oil, you won't be tromping up and down the halls and waking up the rest of us." He took in her astounded expression and grinned mischievously, then relented. "Really, there's a practical reason. The house was modernized several years ago, but we still have our plumbing problems. The plumbing is good enough, if you don't mind taking baths in claw-footed tubs big enough to hold three people. But there is only one bathroom connected to two rooms, if you see what I mean. Sarah and I share one, but then I'm used to her and, anyway, she's not inclined to hang frilly things all around. Mom and Dad have their own bathroom, the only ones who do. Your fiancé will share one with the she-shark, as it stands now, because Carmen insists that she be next to the boss..." He finished lamely, reconsidering what he had been about to say. "We assumed that if someone were found to do the cataloguing, that someone would be male and wouldn't mind sharing a bath with the boss. Now I guess we'll have to switch the boss and Carmen around to keep her happy. We can't afford for her to have fits and quit, but it's a rotten thing to do to a nice girl like you."

He unlocked the storeroom door and turned the knob, pushed it open slightly, and stood back, allowing her to enter first. The room was filled with more of the fabled treasure that her tourists came to find than she thought existed in all the Bahamas put together. Mounds of encrusted, dull greenish coin were stacked, or piled, in one corner, along with chain and pieces of, for now, unidentifiable metal. One entire wall had been devoted to porcelain, stoneware, and crockery, and glassware of every imaginable size, shape, and function, including bags of what she feared were fragments of the same material. Another wall held the dull sheen of gold; not a lot of it, but more than she had ever seen in one place—gold bands, gold containers, delicate gold chain. The collection was astounding and literally took her breath away. If only Rathe hadn't been involved in the project, she thought, she could easily spend three years in seclusion, let alone three months, working on such treasures.

"Well, I know you've had a bit to eat," Ed told her, "but dinner's just about ready, and my mother's a great cook. Let's go down."

Some regrets entered her mind as they headed back to the kitchen, but she knew she had to be firm in her resolve. It would be impossible for her to remain with Rathe. He was sure to try and ruin her relationship with Stavros, and she didn't want that to happen. As she settled into a chair at the kitchen table she was pleased to see that Rathe and Carmen were conspicuously absent.

CHAPTER FIVE

THE BEGINNINGS OF an idea formed in her mind as she excused herself after a fine dinner—made better, she thought wryly, by the absence of Rathe and Carmen.

Everyone turned in early, Ed had said. It should be easy to slip away and parallel the shore until she reached another settlement. Once there, if she couldn't find a way home, she could call her father, who would be more than glad to come for her once he understood the reason. If she were stopped on the way, she could say she had decided to take a look at the boat.

Slipping quietly out of the house, she went along the vine-scented path down the beach and to the docks, for a moment wishing she could commandeer one of the boats. She wouldn't steal from him, though, and stepping into the water, she paralleled the waterline for a ways before turning inland again. The deep beach sand would be apt to slow her progress and, too, she felt vulnerable on the open beach, at least until she'd put some distance between herself and Rathe. For now, inland, with its lush vegetation, would better suit her purpose, providing camouflage for her escape.

The minutes passed and she was forced to admit that in one of her theories she had been wrong. She could have made much better time in the deep sand on shore, because here an abundance of mangrove trees with their tangle of above-ground root systems left hardly any space in which to walk—and that covered with a mesh of climbing vines. The vegetation was rampant, and if she was not tripping over the roots, she was entangled in the often-prickly undergrowth, and before long her arms and hands and face were scratched and dirty, her clothes damp and soiled from her own clumsiness and the moisture, ever present in the mangrove forest.

She stumbled and cried out as her foot caught a root, throwing her down onto the ground. She brushed the humus from her face in frustration. It must be time to turn around and go back to the shore. She sat up and rubbed the bruises that were already forming on her knees. For that matter, it was to be hoped she could find shore again. She stood and turned in a tight little circle, looking this way and that in consternation. She had lost her sense of direction. They sky was no clue; the stars, the moon, indeed, almost all light was hidden from view by the mangroves and their companion trees and plants. A slightly hysterical laugh came to her lips. She had actually been worried that Rathe might track her. The place was a catacomb. Had she escaped one intolerable situation only to land herself in another?

A sound from behind jolted her—footsteps, a crashing, and a snarl that was most definitely not human. She froze like a rabbit which cannot move though it knows the predator is about to spring. It was then she saw it. Small, mean red eyes peered at her stupidly from the shadows; the ugly snout of a boar protruding from the darkness, its white tusks gleaming wickedly in the scant moonlight that filtered through the dense foliage. It snorted, sniffing her scent, and the breath she had heretofore held came out in short, quick sobs. Where was she to hide? Would the animal leave her alone? She had heard stories of men being trampled, mauled, and worse on the boar hunts held on the Abaco Islands. Who would have guessed there were boar on little Andros, too?

There was no time for further speculation, as the animal charged, nimbly dodging the roots in an attempt to reach her. Her screams rent the air and she found the will to move, managing to scramble atop an interlacing of roots that stood three feet or so off the ground before the enraged beast crashed into her perch, shaking the ground with his power and all but dislodging her from the temporary haven.

"Rathe!" She screamed his name, knowing full well that he could not possibly hear her, not knowing if he would care, even if he could hear her, but screaming his name anyway, simply because the cry came from the very depths of her being, from a place within herself over which she had no control.

The boar snorted and turned away from her, only to come once again to ram himself against the mangroves. Had she disturbed his bed, thereby infringing upon his territory, or in some other way threatened him by her presence? It didn't do to wonder further why he might want to reach her. He wanted to, and was pursuing his goal tirelessly. She clung to the mossy, damp surface desperately as he crashed into the tree a third time, breaking one of the smaller, supporting roots in his fury. There were other trees, other high-root systems for her to go to, but in order to reach them, she would have to climb down and run. Would the beast never tire?

"Rathe!" she wailed again and again until the sound echoed in her ears. The boar stopped digging and rooting at the base of her tree, his bristled sides heaving in and out as he panted.

She closed her horrified eyes for a moment, willing the terror that threatened to engulf her to go away. She had never been accused of cowardice, and the years she had spent captaining the tour boat had taught her to be self-reliant. She glanced at the boar again, still resting up for the next onslaught. There might not be another chance. There was no guarantee how much longer her tree refuge could take such abuse and remain stable.

Her heart pounding loudly, she seized the opportunity and jumped, her eyes on a higher platform just a few feet away. But the boar had seen her movement and was charging again, the ground reverberating a quick rat-a-tat-tat as his sharp feet bit into the earth just a few steps behind her.

She touched hard wood, her fingers clawing for a handhold as she pulled herself up. Her feet left the ground, and it wasn't until she felt the contact of tusk against her flesh that she became aware she hadn't quite made the journey in safety. A curious numbing sensation began in the calf of her leg, traveling up to the rest of her body with alarming swiftness until it reached her fingers, which seemed to slip from the wood of their own accord, plunging her to what waited below.

The air whooshed painfully from her lungs as she hit the earth and it was a moment before she could catch her breath. From somewhere just outside her line of vision the boar waited; she could smell the strong, musky odor of his body, hear his labored panting, but there was a ringing in her ears, a radiating pain in her head, and she didn't think she would be able to turn to see him, nor did she want to.

Perhaps she was still stunned, for it seemed to her that time was moving at a curiously slowed pace, the objects in front of her eyes flickering oddly like the pictures one could see at old film festivals; and when Rathe appeared in the foreground, his presence heralded by the beam of a heavy-duty flashlight, her only thought was that his movements were jerky, out of sync. She didn't wonder why he was there—not even truly aware that he *was* there except as a figment of her imagination, a part of her life, flashing before her eyes in the final moments before death. Wasn't it said that one relived one's life at such a time?

She speculated about that, her thoughts frantic until the boar moved into her line of sight and the players on the unusual stage before her began to move faster and faster, as her slowed sense of time caught up with an accelerated reality. The intangible image that was Rathe solidified to become a flesh-and-blood demon, and her

eyes widened in disbelief as he first shined the high-
powered beam into the animal's eyes, momentarily stopping it, then reached with his left hand for a nearby tree
limb on the ground. In transferring it to his right hand,
he dropped the flashlight. So as not to lose his advantage,
he immediately charged the boar, bellowing like a ban-
shee, a primeval berserker intent on destruction.

The boar answered his challenge, snorting and pawing
the earth as he gathered his few wits and enormous
strength together for the counterattack. His tusks gleamed
wickedly in the pale moonlight and he looked more
vicious than before, more desperate now that he had
another foe. The battle commenced and she heard herself
scream as they came together, a cry that was drowned
out as the unintelligible ravings of the man and the
squeals of the beast mingled and echoed off the trees.

It was as if she did not exist for either of them, the
man and the animal facing each other from opposite ends
of the clearing now, medieval jousters awaiting the signal
to resume hostilities. The boar's pink, dull eyes darted
uncertainly about. He had not anticipated being on the
defensive, and unsure whether fight or flight was his best
option he stood quivering and grunting, allowing a moment's respite to Rathe who still stood in waiting, his
muscular legs set in a solid stance of defense, his makeshift weapon clenched in a tight fist. The tension mounted
until she could feel it crackle in the air. The boar felt it
too, his agitated gaze going from Rathe to the forest to
her and back again. She had no intention of remaining
vulnerable while he made his mind up whether to run or
refocus his limited attention back to her, and so she
moved, her legs weak underneath her swaying body, her
only desire to escape the boar who had, it seemed, seen
her furtive movement and reacted to it, shifting its eyes
from the more threatening Rathe to easier prey.

She heard rather than saw Rathe's club crash down
onto the boar's skull, her mind intent on finding a refuge
for herself and not on the struggle going on behind her;

but the winner of that conflict and the footsteps that
chased her were unknown, and as she felt her body hit
the earth, she turned, her eyes and her mind closed to
everything but self-preservation, and she scratched and
kicked out blindly until the fog of terror was penetrated
by the sound of her own name.

"Lorelei . . . Lorelei . . . open your eyes. Damn you,
it's only me. Stop . . . fighting . . . me!"

"Rathe?" She looked wildly about through the tangle
of hair that had fallen over her eyes. "Rathe!" She shook
the curtain of hair aside to reveal him, practically sitting
astride her, his arms locked in a struggle to keep her
hands from inflicting further damage on his face. Sweat
mingled with a small trickle of blood where her nails had
raked his cheek, and it looked as if there were more
marks partially covered by dirt and the lock of hair that
had fallen down over one eye.

"My God, I'm sorry. I thought you were that horrible
pig!"

He scowled deeper. Seeing the fear ebb from her face,
he eased himself from her body and, picking up his
makeshift weapon, walked carefully back toward the
clearing. Rathe seemed satisfied that the animal had fled
the clearing, for taking the dropped flashlight in his hand,
he shone its beam in a last critical scrutiny. He then
disappeared into the forest for further reconnaissance.
He moved through the surrounding vegetation without
sound to come out into the clearing once more only a
few feet from where she lay.

The pig and the danger it represented may have been
gone, but the adrenaline that coursed through Rathe's
veins because of it was not. The muscles of his back and
shoulders and arms were taut and well-defined, even
under the shirt that clung damply to his skin, and he held
himself stiffly, in combat-ready form as he advanced on
her prone figure. Her eyes never left the angry, red
scratches on his finely chiseled face. His expression was
penetrating and icy, without even a hint of warmer
emotion beneath the mask.

What was he thinking? What would he do? He was probably even angrier with her than he had been at the boar, considering that she was responsible for their being in danger in the first place, for their being here at all. Her body shuddered as he dropped the club and refastened those incredibly strong fingers around her shoulders instead. She could feel the heat his body emanated as he knelt beside her, see his chest as it rose and fell heavily, his entire being stimulated from the battle. His whisper was fierce.

"No, you're not next," he said, reading her mind quite accurately. "But you should be."

She didn't doubt he was serious. She had been afraid of him, if only for an instant. She would feel much better if she could only stand and give herself the psychological illusion, however untrue, of being on equal footing with him, but he anticipated the move and tightened his grip on her shoulders, pinning her to the ground.

"Don't move. I have to see how badly you've been hurt."

It didn't sound as though he would care much if she were. "I don't feel very hurt," she interjected.

He cut her off sharply. "Why can't you, for once, just do as you're told? I've seen a man . . . a diver . . . with his entire foot gone from a shark bite, swim to the boat and then swear he wasn't in pain, that he has okay. You could be hurt worse than you imagine, as well. You could be in shock." His voice was gruff, his features uncompromising, but there was an undeniable mixture of strength and gentleness in his fingers and she could feel him trembling as his hands, the hands that had been ready to wrestle with the boar, examined her feet and then her legs as he explored each tendon, each bone, using his fingers like a blind man, relying on his sense of touch for the information he required, until he came to the tear in her denims and heard the involuntary cry that she uttered.

"What happened here?" His steady gray-eyed gaze said: I told you so.

"I think maybe his tusk grazed my leg. I'm not sure, though." She tried to keep from wincing as he probed the wound. "I don't think it's too bad."

He mumbled something under his breath and took the material of her pant leg in his hands, tearing it, exposing her skin from ankle to mid-thigh. "Is that the only place?" Though he questioned her, it was clear he no longer intended to take her word as to whether she was hurt elsewhere.

She hated to admit that he was right. "Yes . . . no . . . that is, I'm sure I'm not cut anywhere else, but my head hurts a little, too. I must have hit it when I fell." She grimaced under his inquisitive fingers. "Really, this isn't necessary," she protested.

He refused to acknowledge her, continuing relentlessly the methodical exploration of her person that would assure him she had no other hidden injuries. His hands moved slowly and thoroughly, and she felt she must only be imagining that his touch took on a more sensuous quality, one that she found herself relaxing under and languishing in, almost unconsciously. Her head spun in circles and she lost track of the meaning of time again as he skillfully ran his hands along her thighs, her hips, touching the slim, smooth lines of her stomach, prodding the bruised area of her ribs.

She sucked in a surprised breath, the strange euphoria fading only a little with the sudden pain. "Don't do that."

"Does it hurt? Does this? What about this over here?" His hands moved slower, searchingly, over her rib cage. His questions were professional and pertained to her physical condition only. She pondered them. It was true, he had found bruised spots she hadn't before been aware of, but mingled with the physical discomfort was a pain from quite a different source. She was unaware that she stared up into his face blankly, her thought processes turned inward. When last this man had held her and explored the whole of her body in such a way, his fingers had sought to discover pleasure and not pain. The old memory was so intense that she writhed away from it, away from him and the hands that cradled her head, from the large, calloused palms that cupped her cheeks and that were being bathed in tears she couldn't stop.

"Don't cry...little runaway, please..." He might have mouthed the words to himself, so softly were they said. Perhaps she had only imagined them, but all of a sudden it no longer mattered that she had been running away from him. She felt curiously lightheaded and it didn't matter that her own arms came up to return his touch. She ran her fingertips along the rugged squareness of his jaw textured with a five o'clock shadow of dark, bristly beard. His eyes no longer viewed her with a clinical, sterile disinterest; they became as obsidian coals, his nostrils flared with some barely controlled emotion, his fingers tangled further in the dark web of her hair. The stream of tears had left streaks of dirt on her face which he wiped at clumsily with his fingers and then, against his will and better judgment, with his lips as he caressed the moist saltiness of her skin, nuzzling her neck, her cheeks. And they still had not spoken. It could have been a dream, like so many other dreams she had shared with him in the past; and as she had done in those dreams, she lifted her head, aggressively seeking his mouth. Only now he did not vanish to leave her alone and frustrated in the darkness of her solitary bed. He was all too real and he returned her embrace with a matching ardor, tasting the inside of her mouth with his tongue, murmuring softly and pressing his long, lean body onto hers so forcefully that she could feel the uneven ground beneath her back, the pressure of his legs as they imprisoned and parted hers.

She wrenched herself away from him and back to reality only with difficulty, pulling the gaping openings of her shirt together in shame and confusion.

He pulled himself together quickly, the raw passion replaced instantly by cynical bitterness. "Are you more afraid to admit that you wanted my loving, started it, and aren't really as much in love with Halkias as you'd like everyone to think?"

"Your loving?" She spat out the word. "You wouldn't begin to know the meaning of the word!"

"Then I would be in like company, my little sea witch, but as to that, I've never had complaints on my ability to love before, and you are beautiful enough, even as you are, to arouse loving thoughts in any man."

"Don't confuse love with lust, Rathe." She glared distastefully at him.

"I don't," he answered flatly. "You're the one who is trying to mingle the two. I can tell you, feeling as you obviously do about me, that your marriage to Halkias just won't work."

Why did he have to be so egotistical? Because he's just been given plenty of reason to believe he's right, her conscience prodded. "The only way I feel about you is sick." She shuddered. He must have sensed the panic in her voice because what she had meant only figuratively was true enough.

Crouching on her knees a short time later she felt no better physically than before, and to top it off, she felt too dizzy to do anything more than remain, unmoving, at the site of her misery. It was one of those times when one wished it were tomorrow and the rest of today could be blotted out, forgotten altogether. Her situation was humiliating in a number of ways, and she must have moaned in anguish, because Rathe moved immediately to her side, oblivious to her frantic protests for him to leave her in peace. He pressed a strip of cloth torn from the hem of his shirt into her hand.

"Sorry, it's all I have at the moment." He sounded surprisingly sympathetic.

A few minutes later, she wiped her face with it gratefully. "I'm sorry you had to use it ... and about before ... that was my fault. I don't know what got into me."

"I do," he responded knowingly. "But I have a feeling if I shared my opinions with you we'd be back at each other's throats again, and right now we need a united front. Can you stand?"

Now came the bad news. "Stand? Maybe. But I'm not so sure about walking back."

He didn't look in the least surprised. "I never intended that you should try to walk back. We won't be going back tonight."

"Pardon?" She couldn't believe her ears. "I can't stay here." This was as inhospitable a place as she had ever been.

"I know how you feel, but there's no way we can go back tonight, if that's what you're hoping." He spoke matter-of-factly.

Had she imagined his sympathy? It was gone, if it had ever existed, replaced by a sullen brooding that was made even more evident by the speed with which he put distance between them, as if he regretted their moments of intimacy as much as she did.

"Why can't we go back?" She stood to follow him but found to her dismay that a sharp, stabbing pain shot up one side of her leg when she tried to put any weight on it, and though she clamped her lips together to prevent Rathe from hearing any sound of groaning, he noticed her discomfort.

"That's why," he said, nodding curtly at her leg. "We can get to the beach and away from all these insects and stagnant water, but that's about as far as I think we can make it tonight." He watched her closely. "Okay, let me see your leg now. I don't think it's too badly hurt but my examination was . . . postponed."

He ignored the flush that colored her face and held the fabric of her torn denims apart, turning her body a bit to illuminate the wound, still partially concealed in the shadows. He squinted at it seriously.

"It isn't deep, but you can't walk on it tonight. It really needs a stitch or two, but failing that, a few hours of staying off it will probably do the trick and close it up."

"You're sure?" she questioned him anxiously.

"I'm not a doctor, if that's what you mean, but even I can tell walking won't do you any good. Take my word for it, will you?"

She would have to; there wasn't any choice. She rubbed the side of her temple, which had begun to ache abominably.

"Don't look like that, Lorelei. I can't carry you back to the plantation and you can't convince me to try by looking like a whipped puppy. I had more than enough trouble keeping up with you."

"You followed me?" she asked in surprise. Of course, he would have had to in order to hear her cries for help. He hadn't simply materialized out of thin air. "I didn't hear you; I didn't hear anything until the boar came crashing out of the trees."

"Mmmmm, yes, well that's not surprising." He chuckled. "You're about as quiet as a Sherman tank . . . or another adult boar, which is probably what our porker friend thought you were. He was defending his territory against the only thing that could possibly make that much noise."

She didn't see the humor in his remark and threw him a cold, withering glance, one gleaned from her navy vice-admiral father's repertoire of authoritative looks, but it didn't have the desired effect—in fact, he only laughed all the louder, a mocking, unfriendly sound that made her grit her teeth in frustration. If she didn't feel so absolutely terrible she'd. . . . As it was, she turned her head to ignore him.

She was relieved to hear that he had stopped laughing, but the jeering, self-satisfied expression would still be there, she knew. She could see it in her mind's eye and she had to turn around to look at him, in spite of herself, just to make sure. He obviously thought the whole miserable business was just what she deserved. The more she thought about it, the angrier she became until, finally, she reacted with all the fury she could muster.

"How dare you sit there and smirk at me. I could have been killed."

He nodded sagely with a smug gleam. "And would have been, too, if I hadn't heard you raising all holy hell, and it would have been your own fault. But, Lorelei, out of curiosity, why did you yell for me and not for your knight in shining Greek armor?"

She answered him quickly—he *would* have to remember something like that. "You were uppermost in my mind." No, that hadn't been what she meant to say. "What I mean is that it was your fault. If you had allowed me to leave by any normal means, it wouldn't have happened. If you had stopped me when you knew I was headed into this . . . this awful place, it wouldn't have happened, so I yelled for you because it was all your fault." The explanation didn't make a bit of sense. In truth, she didn't know why she had called out his name in that moment of panic.

"You had time to think all that, did you?" he scoffed. Then, on a sharper note, he probed further. "Why did you really leave?"

"Why didn't you stop me?" she countered.

"I believe I asked you the first question." He waited for her answer in vain. "Stubborn woman. I didn't stop you because I wanted to see what you would do, where you would go. Call it a test."

"A test that could very well have gotten me killed," she shrilled.

"I didn't force you to leave, or make the rules once you did. I was an observer, nothing more." He tapped his fingers against his knee. "Surely you realized there would be risks to setting out all alone, at night, through the forest, on an island not only unfamiliar to you, but one that is all but unexplored in the direction you were headed."

"The risks seemed slight compared to spending three months on Andros with you. What did you intend to do . . . let me blunder on indefinitely?"

"No," he answered, "I would have stopped you before you hit the mud shallows."

"I wasn't that far inland?" The west side of the forty-mile-wide island was all but totally unexplored, in part because of the mud shallows that kept boats at a distance, in part because the east coast that they were on had so much more to offer in the way of recreation—and no one took the time to explore an area that didn't seem to be as readily enjoyable.

He nodded. "You were headed that way, and you had to pick an escape route through a stand of mangroves. Most of the island is pine, and brush—not easy walking, in and of itself; but in a few places there are the mangroves and no one goes through them by choice."

"I don't believe my luck lately—first you and then the boar and now this . . ." She frowned at the misshapen ugly trees with their roots all above ground, looking as if they might lift their legs and walk away at any moment.

"Tell me why you were leaving, Lorelei, and why you decided to come this way," he persisted. "I saw you go to the docks first. Did you see me? Is that why you changed your mind, or had you already done whatever it was you set out to do there?"

"Changed my mind?" she echoed. "About what? I was leaving the plantation, leaving the island if I could. I didn't see you, or anyone else anywhere. I can't think what you're talking about."

He was angry; she could hear it in his voice. "Oh, I know what I'm talking about all right, and I think you do too. I think you went to see if you could find a way to interfere with this project . . . wreck some equipment . . . damage a boat, anything to hurt me just a little more. I think you saw me following you, and that's why you called out my name when the boar attacked. I think it's the only reason you would go into the mangroves. You hoped to lose me, and I don't think you can deny it."

He wouldn't believe her, no matter what she said— that much was evident—but so far he hadn't given her a moment to get in a word in her own defense.

"I *was* trying to make sure you couldn't follow me, yes," she admitted. "But not because I thought you were following me, only because I know you well enough to know you would try. You can't stand it when everything doesn't go your own way, but you must be mad if you think I would deliberately try to sabotage your project. I would never interfere with you or your precious project other than to get as far away from it, and you, as possible. In fact, I thought you were in your bedroom when I left. I was sure you wouldn't be thinking about me when you had Car—" She took several deep breaths. "It doesn't matter where I thought you were. The point is, my only goal was to get away from you."

"It *does* matter, it has to!" he thundered at her. "I have no choice but to keep you on this island for three long months, and it matters one hell of a lot whether all I have to do is keep an eye on you so that you don't leave or whether I have to find a way to keep an armed guard on you to prevent you from destroying everything I have worked so hard these past years to achieve."

The pent-up energy welled up inside him, forcing him to get up, to do something. He paced back and forth. When he sat down again, Lorelei thought he looked uncomfortable.

"I would really like to believe you. It would give me a little peace of mind; but you forget, I've been the victim of your lies and your revenge before, and I just can't take your word on anything. You lie quite well."

Surely he couldn't be referring to the lies she had told him that day in front of her father, that she only thought of him as a summer romance and nothing more. He had gone and then made no effort to contact her, and she felt he would have done so if he had realized she loved him. He'd have tried to convince her to come away with him and live, as her Old World in-laws-to-be would have put it, in sin. No, he could not be aware of that deception, but other than that, she had never lied to him.

"Rathe, no matter what you think of me, you must know I would never be so vengeful as to destroy another person's property, and I don't know why you think I would. I have never given you a reason to think I'd interfere with your salvage projects. Why, there was a time when I was every bit as involved in them, as anxious for the outcome, as you were. You must remember that."

"I remember you *seemed* to be, but it was only another of your games, wasn't it?" he queried bitterly. "I don't suppose you consider it vengeful that all my financing was cut off at a crucial stage in the research? You wouldn't consider that interference?"

She felt bewildered, but his only reaction to the look of shock that she knew must be on her face was to continue to address her in a sarcastic voice. "Don't pretend you didn't know. Your father cut off all research funds to my project the day we broke off our . . . relationship."

"But he financed your first salvage expedition, and we were lucky. I remember—" She bit her lip to stop the flow of words, changing the ending of what she had been about to say. "I remember him saying you had a brilliant future ahead of you. He used to say that you had a positively uncanny knack for locating wrecks, a sort of biological metal detector. He used to brag that you and he were like two peas in a pod . . .

"Heaven forbid . . ." Rathe muttered.

"Why would he simply cut off your financing?"

"Why indeed, Lorelei, unless *you* had something to do with it. You can't blame me for thinking along those lines, can you?"

"But you must have spoken to him about it and asked for a reason?"

His answer was cryptic. "He refused to see me or answer my calls."

"But that doesn't make sense. My father isn't arbitrary. For him, everything goes by the book. Personal feelings don't enter into his decisions. He weighs matters logically and acts accordingly. If he thought your project had a chance of success, and if that success would have benefited him, I can't think of a single reason why he would cancel his financial backing. How can I convince you that neither his personal feelings nor mine would have influenced that decision?"

"You can't. I believe he withdrew his support because he didn't want me around you, and you agreed, for the same reasons, and perhaps you were right. A simple 'Rathe, get lost,' wouldn't have worked. Our relationship had progressed too far, and I hold on to what is mine. By running away tonight, you've only proven my theory. You didn't care how it would affect me, your breaking contract, you simply left. Can you blame me for wondering what else you might do to gain your own ends? If you have no qualms about breaking contracts, violating security, what do you hold sacred?"

"That's a lousy thing to say." She was appalled. "It's not fair."

"I've found that very little in life is fair, Lorelei. You taught me that lesson the hard way. Perhaps you're a victim of karma. You reap what you sow."

"Whatever happened to turning the other cheek, if we're talking in parables?" Her green eyes met his gray ones for a long moment, then she looked away with a sigh. "No, never mind. I'm sure you'd have some smart answer for that too. So you intend to put me on probation? If everything goes right, I'll be vindicated, is that right? Or do you never intend to trust me? Will you dwell on me for the whole of my three-month stay on Andros, waiting for me to prove your suspicions right?"

He looked haggard and weary. "I've dwelled on you, as you put it, for a long time. Another three months won't make any difference one way or another. However, I doubt even you could cause me more trouble tonight, so as soon as we get down to the beach, I intend to sleep. If I'm lucky, I won't think of you at all."

The driftwood fire popped and crackled comfortingly and, though she was almost asleep, through her half-

open lids she could see the outline of Rathe's body as
he lay across the fire from her. His eyes were half-open
too, and she wondered what he thought of as he stared
back at her through the flames. Probably he was missing
his large comfortable bed and the woman he'd left behind
in it. Sharing the night with Carmen would be much
nicer than this, especially when *this* meant only the hard
sand for a bed and the company of a woman he neither
liked nor trusted. She longed to ask him if she were right,
but he did not seem inclined to talk, so she rolled over
onto her other side. The fire now warmed her backside.
She shivered and inched closer to the fire and its light,
then crabbed her way back again as she felt her skin
become too warm.

"Lorelei," Rathe mumbled in irritation. "Is there some
reason for you to be squirming over there or are you
purposely trying to prevent me from getting to sleep?"

He would believe the worst! "Sorry," she whispered
apologetically. Somehow when someone mentioned
something you were doing, like a nervous tick, a habit,
or...or...squirming, it focused your attention on it,
making it impossible to stop. She moved over a bit,
trying not to be obvious that she was doing so.

"Is it that you need to go to the bathroom and are
afraid to go alone?" Rathe's voice was full of sarcasm,
and when she turned over to look at him, the first thing
she noticed was his wide-awake eyes and vaguely annoyed expression. The second thing was a pair of red-
pink eyes in the forest behind him, at the edge of the
beach. She gasped.

"What? Where? What is it?" He turned in circles and
then came over to her, pulling her hands from her face.
She pointed through the fire.

"I saw him. I swear I saw that pig again, or his eyes
anyway. Rathe, he is over there. Would he charge down
onto the beach after us?"

"Hush, Lorelei, hush. That pig is long gone and he
wouldn't rush us here. All you saw were the sparks from
the fire."

"Oh, great!" She sat up, marveling at her own stupidity. "I feel absolutely ridiculous. I am not prone to hysteria or being afraid of boogeymen." She hastened to reassure him, saying, "My encounter with that boar must have been more traumatic than I realized. I could have sworn I saw something."

He ran a hand over his tired face, licked his lips, and let out a long sigh. "And I just said even you couldn't cause me more trouble tonight. Live and learn. Have you heard the chickcharnie legends?"

She looked doubtful, but her sense of humor, dormant throughout most of this episode, resurfaced. "Chickcharnies? Are they horrible hungry beasties whom you plan to feed me to if I don't let you get some sleep?"

"It's not a bad idea." A muscle twitched in the corner of his mouth. "Actually, they're our answer to the Irish leprechaun. They're tiny elves, *red*-eyed—" he emphasized the word, "—tree-dwelling gremlins. They're reputed to live in the island pines, but you never know, we might have a band of them living in the suburbs, nesting in our mangroves and above these slight sand dunes. They are said to be a great force for good or evil if you see one of them. Which is it going to be with you?"

"Good." She prayed fervently. "It's my turn for some good luck."

"Then I wish I'd see one." He crawled back to his own place by the fire. "Are you sure you want to spend the night on the other side of the fire with the chickcharnies and whatever other things that might go bump in the night?"

"I think I'm more capable of dealing with any of those things than I am dealing with you," she said dryly.

"I do hope so, because if you wake me up once more you're going to have to deal with me and live with the consequences."

The words were serious but his tone had lightened considerably. He was such a complex man, angry and threatening one minute, the next, almost teasing. It was as if he didn't know quite how he wanted to treat her and was at war with himself over the uncertainty. She could only hope he would eventually decide in her favor, and somehow they could try to work out an armed truce, if not a true friendship. Friendship—she savored the thought. No. She couldn't even imagine having a luke-warm, platonic relationship with a man like Rathe. It would be impossible; one either loved or hated him. And she was determined that she would not allow herself to love him, only to be hurt, again. Perhaps they could learn to tolerate each other, though. Two adult, profes-sional people should be able to manage that, shouldn't they?

"Have you decided where you're going to sleep?"

"Yes, I'll be fine right here, thank you."

He nodded his acceptance, but he knew why she had come to that decision. "Sweet dreams then, Lorelei."

She went to sleep with the heat of the fire and the picture of his figure across from it scorched into her mind, and her dreams were sweet, but they weren't of Stavros.

CHAPTER SIX

THE EARLY MORNING sunshine felt delicious on her skin but was still not enough to dispel the chilly, damp feeling caused by sleeping all night out on the open beach. Lorelei rose and took a few tentative steps in the direction of the water. Her leg wound was hot and aching. But it was a sparkling day, one that made the spirit soar, and she stretched her stiff limbs languorously.

She was covered with dew. Rathe was too, but he didn't seem to be bothered by it, perhaps too worn out from the night before to care whether he slept wet or dry, as long as he slept.

She whirled as her peripheral vision picked up movement and was surprised to see Rathe up and collecting driftwood. "Good morning," she said. Her greeting was tentative, as she couldn't be sure what kind of a mood he might be in this morning.

"Morning," he replied, with a voice still thick with sleep. "How's the leg?"

"Not too bad." She stretched the leg in question, testing its tenderness, finding it much improved from even a few minutes ago and much better than the night before. "I just walked on it a little. The stiffness is working out, I think. My headache is gone too," she added in surprise. "But my ribs aren't going to be pretty." She lifted the edge of her shirt to inspect the bruises that looked only slightly worse than they felt.

Rathe frowned at the pale blue marks. "I didn't feel any obvious breaks, but—"

"Not to worry, nothing's broken," she assured him, dropping the edge of her shirt. "I know all about these things, from painful firsthand experience." She ran a hand through her tangled hair, the best she could do without a comb. "A couple of years ago I was running on deck, a no-no in the first place, to rescue a woman tourist who tried to chase her fish and fishing tackle overboard. You know the type, can't bear to have a big one get away. Anyway, she was hanging off the stern by her toes when I saw her; I made a mad dash and slipped and fell, cracking a few ribs. Believe me—" she touched her ribs gingerly, "—these aren't anywhere near that uncomfortable."

"Maybe." He remained unconvinced. "But all the same, I'd like to get you to the island doctor for a professional look, just to be on the safe side."

"I didn't know Andros had a resident doctor. Wouldn't that violate your contract . . . the no-contact-with-the-outside-world clause?"

She only said it as a joke, but he took her remark seriously and snapped, "The contract is a formality which I expect my employees to respect, as it's in their best interests as well as mine, but it isn't ironclad in all circumstances, particularly not in medical emergencies . . . even for you. Give me a little credit for common sense, if not for my humanity." He lifted the watch on his arm impatiently and glowered at it though she had the distinct impression the look was meant for her.

"We have to get going. I don't want to have the folks at the plantation more worried about us than necessary. I'd hoped to be back before we were missed, but failing that I want to get back before they have a mainland search party combing the island for us. Do you feel up to it?"

"I don't suppose I have much choice," she retorted dryly.

"I could carry you the entire distance, in the daylight, but I would much rather not." The prospect was a distasteful one, if the sour look on his face was any sign.

"I can walk." It remained to be seen how far... but she *could* walk and was resigned to do so without his aid. After less than a mile, however, she realized her limitations. The fine gritty sand clung to her wet feet and to the wet material of her pants, working its way insidiously into every crack and crevice and cranny, grating on her skin and into the gash on her leg that had come open from all the exertion.

The salty water stung and burned and she had to slow her pace several times. No longer determined to keep up with Rathe, her only goal was to keep going, somehow. Rathe was well ahead of her, easily outdistancing her with his long-legged stride, but he finally turned to watch her hobble, huffing and puffing, walking crablike through the ankle-deep sand, each step fast becoming more difficult than the last. If he had been anyone else, she would have given in and begged for help. If he had been anyone else, she fumed silently, help would have been offered long ago and she'd not have to beg for it. As it was, she'd walk, even if it took her the rest of the day to reach the plantation. She gritted her teeth, commanding her aching body to respond to her willful mind.

He surveyed her ash-pale face and set mouth critically. "You have a choice, Lorelei, but I'm going to have to carry you whether you like it or not."

That was out— o-u-t, out! "I do *not* want to be carried," she protested. "Aren't we almost there?"

"Yes, we have about three-quarters of a mile to go, but that isn't the choice you have, whether to walk or not."

"Three-quarters of a mile!" She echoed forlornly, not caring that her exclamation gave away her stoic pride. How could she have possibly walked that far last night?

"I can carry you in a fireman's carry or—"

She knew what that entailed. "No, and I mean it,

Rathe. I will not ride like a sack of potatoes thrown over
your shoulder." She hobbled backward as he advanced,
almost tripping over a half-submerged piece of driftwood.

"It would be easier on your ribs."

"But not on my dignity. No, and that's final. Rathe,
please." She eyed him distrustingly. It would be entirely
in character for him to sweep her up and toss her over
his shoulder. He was proving himself to be a man of
very little patience or empthy.

He chuckled; he was enjoying her predicament again.
"Come on, Lorelei, who's going to see you?"

"You will, and I'm sure I can walk. I'll get there; just
give me a little time." Damn the man, he knew he had
the winning hand.

"You're only under contract for three months and
there is a lot of work to do. I want you to spend most
of it working, not walking back and/or recovering."

"Don't be absurd!"

"Then don't be stubborn." She felt the strain ease up
on her legs as her feet left the ground and she struggled
to remain upright by clinging to his neck, but he appeared
to have no intention of carrying her, bottom-end up, as
she feared, but settled her sore ribs against his chest
instead, supporting her weight with a firm hold under
her legs and arms. Her head rested, not uncomfortably,
against the material of what was left of his shirt, her long
dark hair blowing in the soft sea breeze. She decided not
to fight the contact, and allowed the fabric to brush
against her cheek as he walked.

Rathe's grip on her tightened protectively. "I think
we have company . . . wake up. Are you ready to face
the music?"

Well, ready or not, she had to be, because the crew
members were streaming off the verandah of the plantation and heading swiftly toward them. Stavros, Lorelei
noted, had come back.

"What happened?"

"Is she all right?"

"Where have you been?"

The questions came out in a jumble of confusion as everyone spoke at the same time, preventing any exchange of information above the roar.

"Quiet!" Rathe demanded and was instantly obeyed. She didn't know whether to be grateful or annoyed.

"You can put me down now. We're here." She muttered the words to Rathe under her breath but Stavros heard them and stepped forward, his arms outstretched.

"Or give her to me. You must be exhausted, both of you."

Rathe did not deny it but she could feel his chest and arm muscles contract and she thought that he gave up his self-imposed burden reluctantly, but then she realized that impression was crazy. He hadn't wanted to carry her in the first place.

She leaned heavily against Stavros, supported by his comforting arms. "Don't look so concerned," she whispered to him. "I'm fine, honestly."

As if to deny her statement, Rathe spoke quickly. "Taylor, bring the jeep around, pronto. I'm taking Miss Averill in to see the doctor."

"No, Rathe, I don't need to." She touched his forearm.

Rathe's eyes flickered to Stavros. "Your fiancé is a very stubborn woman, Halkias."

It was not a friendly, joking kind of comment, but Stavros, bless his positive attitude, attributed it to worry on Rathe's part, though Lorelei knew differently.

"You should try living with her twenty-four hours a day." Stavros laughed then cleared his throat, correcting himself. "What I mean is, she has a tour boat and I've spent a few weekends on it, with friends, and there's no doubt who the captain is."

Lorelei held her breath, sure that Rathe would let the cat out of the bag and tell everyone he had spent an entire summer on Lorelei's boat...not always with friends. But he did not. Instead, he lifted his eyebrows suggestively.

"At least she's picked a career that suits her personality." He was mentally adding "bossy," she knew, but Stavros didn't.

"Yes, indeed. It takes a special kind of woman to be able to captain a boat and handle tourists all at the same time." He smiled at Lorelei and lifted her up. "Enough of that for now. We need to get you inside, sweetheart, then you can tell us all what happened. We were all pretty worried."

"Pretty worried?" Ed chimed in. "You should have heard Carmen when she heard you hadn't made it back."

"I'll bet," Lorelei muttered under her breath. From there the questions escalated, and later, over the huge breakfast Lucy had cooked hastily, Lorelei wondered how she would have gotten through it all without Rathe. She had decided last night and on the way back that she wouldn't tell Stavros the whole story. She believed in honesty as a general rule, but in this situation, no good could come from purging her conscience and being one-hundred-percent truthful. Though they hadn't discussed it, Rathe apparently agreed and concocted a plausible story about her being caught unawares by the boar during a late evening stroll and chased into the mangroves. Hearing her first startled cries, Rathe had come and followed her as she ran in blind panic through the forest; then, upon catching up to her and seeing that she was hurt, he decided they should camp on the beach for the night.

Basically it was true, except for the motivation behind her so-called late evening stroll, and his leaving out just how far they had been from the plantation. But no one seemed inclined to question it, save Carmen Alvarada, and she with only her large expressive eyes that quite clearly said, to Lorelei, no woman could spend a night alone with such a man and just sleep. Heaven alone knew what she might have said aloud concerning her suspicions if Taylor had not changed the subject to one closer and more interesting to them all.

"Went down to the wreck early this morning, Rathe,"

he said. Plainly a man who didn't like to be hurried until he had his audience's full attention, Taylor then took a cigar from his shirt pocket. After a shared glance and a nod of approval from Lucy, he lit the cheroot and settled back comfortably in the dining room chair.

"You didn't go alone?" Rathe asked disapprovingly.

The old man nodded. "Had to. Everyone else was out looking for you two."

"But not you, Taylor?"

"I knew you'd turn up." He grunted and held up a gnarled hand. "And I know you don't like me going under alone, but 'twas an area I know well and have dived in alone since long before you owned a pair of swimming pants, so don't look down your nose and preach safety at me. Besides, I found something that makes it worthwhile."

Rathe studied the old man silently for a moment. "Tell me what you found."

"Not what I've found, but what I think I've found."

"Tell me!" There were times when the old man's careful, meticulous patience and deliberate snail's pace were an asset, but this was not one of them.

He spoke, finally. "I went to the wreck to collect the bag of things we found yesterday—and, yes, I know we should bring them up every day, and that's why I went down alone this morning, to bring them in before you returned." Taylor looked sheepish, then puffed hurriedly on the foul-smelling cigar. Lorelei could tell that he found it difficult to have to answer to anyone.

"Go on." Rathe didn't refer to the bag of artifacts, forgotten offshore the night before.

"In my hurry, I swam over one of them blue holes and . . . I dropped the bag . . . straight down." He pursed his lips and made a whistling sound and pointed down to the floor for effect.

"You didn't," Rathe said flatly.

"Well, and that's how I knew you'd feel about it, and so I went in after it."

"You didn't."

Even Lorelei gasped at that. Andros's great barrier reef was in itself safe enough and attracted many divers, the depth of its water only some twelve to twenty feet, until one came to the spectacular "tongue of the ocean," which dropped off to over a mile. But dotted seemingly innocuously here and there throughout the reef were the blue holes, far into which divers with any sense did not venture alone. A diving problem at twelve feet without a buddy nearby might be one thing, but the same problem in a deep hole of jagged coral was another altogether.

Rathe was angry now and was not holding it back to save the old man's pride. "The damn things go down two hundred feet, some of them—you know that, Taylor—and narrow to where even your scrawny body couldn't turn around. That coral is razor sharp..."

Taylor didn't let him finish. "I figured maybe the bag had snagged on an outcropping, close to the surface or lodged on a shelf. It hadn't," he added as an afterthought. "But I saw something else that did, something that could be far more valuable."

"I don't care if you found the crown jewels of England in that hole, do you hear me, Taylor Yates? I don't want to see you as fish bait. You will not dive down in there alone again, not and work for me you won't!"

"And so we told him." Lucy had slid unobtrusively in behind her husband, her plump hands resting on his shoulders. "It was a fool thing to do."

"But listen, listen, Rathe, to what he found." Ed all but hopped up and down in excitement, his youthful face animated by the knowledge he obviously shared.

"Do let him get it out, darling. It's been 'secret city' all morning. They won't tell anyone." Anyone meaning Carmen, obviously, who had so far removed herself from their conversation, smoking her cigarette and drinking her coffee in stony silence, the only one who had not forgotten the earlier excitement.

"You did find the crown jewels?" Having made his

point about safety, Rathe lightened his manner and the atmosphere in the room along with it.

"I didn't have a good look-see, mind, but I saw a little boat down on a shelf, turned over on its side, rotted in places, and through the holes, a box. It looked to be the right age that we're looking for."

"I know what you're getting at," Rathe said.

"What I'm wondering is if some of the sailors didn't try to jump ship, before she went down, taking with them some of the best cargo?" Taylor finished provocatively.

Rathe fingered his chin thoughtfully. "It's true we haven't found some of the best items that should be down there. I suppose it's possible some of those seamen tried to save the valuables along with themselves."

"Aye, I agree." Taylor nodded sagely.

"And you say this boat is sitting on a shelf, about how far down?"

Taylor shrugged. "Hard to say for sure, but we should be able to deal with it with just our own crew."

Rathe murmured his agreement. "I would hate to bring in any extra people, and I don't want to take the time to go for more sophisticated equipment unless we absolutely need it."

"Can we look at it today? How do you plan to bring it up?" Clearly Ed favored the idea of looking at it immediately, if not sooner, and if it were up to him, they'd all no doubt be in diving suits now. Eager and excited, he resembled a kid on Christmas morning.

Sarah and Lucy quickly cleared the table of dishes which were rapidly replaced by maps and graphs, diagrams, and writing implements, and surrounded by the crew who, in this one thing at least, were one-hundred-percent together, their attitude professional, their concentration on the task ahead total. Lorelei felt more than a little left out. Not having yet been fully briefed on the details, she knew less about what they hoped to find than Stavros, who was firmly wedged between Carmen's statuesque body and Ed's as they crowded around the table.

"Do you know what may be in the box, Rathe?" Carmen breathed his name in a husky, familiar way, making Lorelei wonder nastily how many times she'd practiced saying it to achieve that sultry effect.

"Maybe." Rathe nodded. "But I would rather not say anything yet. *If* the craft was from the galleon, launched just before she broke up on the reef, the crew might have been practical—fishing gear, tools—"

"Or they might not have been practical," finished Carmen. There were greedy inflections in her voice. But what did she stand to gain even if there was a king's ransom in the little boat? Lorelei wondered. The answer leaped to mind. The treasure was Rathe's; as his wife, Carmen would have an equal share in all that was found. The thought was repugnant. . . . She left quickly.

She snapped on the bathroom light and glanced at the door that connected Rathe's bedroom to their shared bathroom, then locked it securely before closing her own connecting door. She drew the torn denims from her leg gingerly, inspecting it as best she could, bending backward and peering over her shoulder. It didn't look too bad, long-distance, but try as she might, she couldn't twist her body around to better investigate it, and so, banking on the out-of-sight, out-of-mind theory, she gave up the effort. She turned on the taps and put a generous supply of bath salts into the bathtub. It was to be hoped Rathe's plantation house had an extra-large water heater, because she planned to fill the tub up to its luxurious limits.

This done, she left her hair free to become saturated in the foamy bathwater and climbed in, flinching at first as the hot water made contact with her skin. She couldn't remember the last time she had pampered herself with a long, leisurely bubble bath. Usually she had only a dip overboard with a bar of soap and a quick towel dry, or a short navy shower, taken out of habit rather than necessity. It would be so easy to slip down and doze . . .

The water splashed and the door clicked open almost

at the same time and Lorelei opened her eyes and plucked the teaspoon from the water at her feet.

"Drop something?" She raised one dripping hand and the teaspoon from the water and handed it back to Lucy. My, this was a friendly family.

"Oh, I'm sorry. I brought you some tea, and I did knock, but you must have fallen asleep."

"I must have." Lorelei yawned and added dryly, "I didn't get much sleep last night." Then, "Thanks for the tea, Lucy."

"No bother at all, and by the way, I was sure you'd want to go down to the beach with the others to see the new discovery, so I saved you the trouble and unpacked your clothes. There's a very nice pair of orange shorts and a tangerine tee shirt all laid out for you on the bed. And, dear, I'll be upstairs cleaning the rooms for a bit more, so if you need anything more just holler out."

Lorelei sipped the tea with pleasure, slowly, taking the cup from her lips when she heard a knock at the door. Lucy again, probably.

"Come in," she yelled and gulped down the remains of the tea, holding the empty cup in one hand and the saucer in the other, ready to hand them back to Lucy . . . then she realized that the person standing in the open doorway was not, most definitely not, Lucy. The lean, tanned legs that could be seen from under black swim trunks and the naked torso with its covering of fine, dark hair was too familiar.

"What is this, Grand Central Station?" she shouted and glared up at a faintly amused Rathe. "You'd think I was holding a real-estate open house here!"

He shrugged apologetically but made no move to leave. "You did say to come in." His eyes took in her unclothed body, covered in a thin layer of bath bubbles.

She sank lower in the tub, grateful for its high-sided construction. Blast the subtle approach. "Will you please leave!" she demanded.

"Not until we've talked." He shook his head.

It helps to count to ten, Lorelei, she commanded herself. "I really can't have an intelligent conversation with someone in my bathroom." She was being as sweet and as polite as she could, and the strain was killing her.

"Oh, I agree," he said sagely. "I couldn't begin to have...an intelligent conversation—" he arched one eyebrow, "—with someone lying prone in a bubble bath. So why don't you come out?"

"I had planned to do just that before you barged your way in here, so if you leave, I'll get out now."

He clucked his tongue regretfully. "I couldn't do that, Lorelei, you might slip away again, and if I do say so, you look slippery enough to do it."

"Stop trying to be cute and *get out!*" she demanded loudly, then softened her voice as she remembered that Lucy was still upstairs. She groaned...Lucy. "Rathe, Lucy is up here cleaning and I expect her in here any minute. Will you please leave before she comes?" Her voice held real pleading this time.

"That depends." He smiled. "I'm waiting."

Why did he have to be so impossibly stubborn and so damned impractical? Being the boss, he probably didn't care what his domestic help thought of his morals, but she had no such indifference. She liked Lucy and, besides, this was hardly the ideal place to hold a conversation. It was *not* the ideal place at all, she knew it as soon as Lucy's quick tapping footsteps turned from the hallway into her bedroom. Without further thought, she leaped from the tub and slammed the door, leaning against it in anxiety.

"You have got to get out of here now before she decides to make a surprise inspection," she whispered.

"I can't walk on air, she'd hear me." He looked absolutely unconcerned.

"Then for heaven's sake, hide," she hissed frantically.

"In there?" He pointed to the tub teasingly.

He looked so self-satisfied that if he had dared to get near the tub she could have cheerfully drowned him. She

closed her eyes, counting to her second set of ten with
equally unhelpful results, and by the time she opened
them it was to find that he had moved, to within inches
of her. He reached past her to lock the door.

"Miss Lorelei, are you all right? You haven't fallen
asleep again?"

"Yes, I'm doing fine," she answered back while grab-
bing a towel and draping it in front of her. "I'll be out
in a minute."

"Do you want your clothes, dear?" The helpful voice
came again.

Oh, *did* she want her clothes. . . . "No, thank you,
Lucy." She forced herself to lie. "I don't need them
now."

Rathe raised an eyebrow again, silently suggestive,
making her even more conscious of her nakedness as
Lucy's footsteps echoed down the hall and faded into
nothing as she reached the carpeted stairway.

"Please, Rathe . . . there's no point in this."

It seemed for a moment that he might let her go, as
if he agreed, his gray eyes showing regret then something
else as his arms came around to rest lightly on her hips.
She found herself unable to move, her will draining away
impotently along with the soap bubbles to a puddle on
the floor.

"Please what? Please let you go? You don't mean
that." His voice was husky and low and he pulled her
closer so that the towel fell away and the tips of her
breasts rubbed against his chest. Her breath came fast,
from the confusion, from the near confrontation, from
embarrassment, she told herself. But there was no explanation as she felt her nipples grow hard and press into
his flesh, just as she knew there was no way the physical
proof of her arousal could escape his attention. She tried
to block the urges her body was trying to send to her
mind, if all else failed, to say or do something, anything
to make him leave.

"It's no good, Lorelei. You can't lie to me . . . not to

me. No matter what you tell everyone else, I know who you are and what you are underneath that windswept exterior everyone else is trying so hard to polish."

"I don't know what you're trying to say and, furthermore, I don't care. Let me go."

"You don't seriously intend to marry this Halkias fellow, do you, my little mermaid?" His hands caressed her skin with a butterfly touch.

"Yes, I do and I don't know why that should seem so strange to you. He's a good man, kind and gentle, and he loves me enough to offer marriage."

"And lots of security?" he asked softly.

"Yes," she said, trying to twist away from his fingers which were becoming more demanding, "which was more than you ever offered me." Having a simple conversation with the man was like playing chess. He put her instantly on the defensive.

"Not more," he countered. "Just different."

"Better."

"Better? And does what he gives you compensate for this?" She found herself molded to his body, her back pressed so tightly between the door and his enveloping arms that she could scarcely breathe.

"I am not kind..." she heard him murmur thickly, "nor am I always gentle, and by God, I'll offer no woman more than I once offered you, but tell me now, if you can, that what he gives you is better than what I give you, better than how I make you feel when I touch you." He kissed her, draining away her resistance. She had to leave soon, she knew, or make him leave before she gave way to the desire that raged within her like a caged animal.

Her voice was low and panicky. "If you don't let me go, this instant, I swear I'll start screaming now and I won't stop until I have the entire house up here. I know you don't want that kind of trouble, because if I am forced to do that, both Stavros and I leave, contract or no contract, and your precious secrets go with us."

His eyes hardened bitterly. "What a pity you don't hold the same financial club over my head that your father once did. You could use that too."

Would that she could have some weapon to use against him. He might hate her with his mind, with his heart, but his body was as traitorous as hers and was insistently demanding fulfillment. She pushed him away with all the will she could muster, which wasn't much.

"There are other ways to make trouble for a person. Don't force my hand, Rathe. Let me go." He did, but she hadn't won a victory.

"That's a sword that cuts both ways," he threatened. "You can tell Halkias or anyone else anything you like about this project, but hear this: I'm not bound and gagged by my emotions anymore. I wouldn't hesitate to use every detrimental scrap of information I know or could make up about you to safeguard the security of this operation. I'm sure you don't want either Halkias or his family to know the extent of our relationship . . . past and present. . . . Think how difficult it would be for him to work with me then. If you break contract, I can take you to court, both of you, and then the story would get out anyway, and I happen to know your respectable Greek in-laws-to-be already disapprove of your somewhat avant-garde way of living."

She blanched. "Stavros values his family ties very highly. To have to chose between them and me would destroy him."

"And you might not come out the winner. So, that's what should concern you and govern your impulsive actions. I assure you, if anything you do interferes with what I want . . . well, I won't be the only loser, this time. Do I make my intentions perfectly clear?"

"Your *blackmail*, do you mean?"

"Call it whatever you like. You do understand?"

"Yes." She did, all too well.

He opened the door, allowing a cool breeze to enter the steamy confines of the room. She hadn't intended to threaten him, it had just happened. She wouldn't even dream of exposing his secrets; that would be unethical. But what he had done to her senses was unethical too, and she had been able to think of no other way to force him to leave... and if he had stayed, she would have lost what little pride and dignity remained to her as far as he was concerned, and she would have given him yet another weapon to hold over her head.

She couldn't tell Stavros about Rathe's actions today without giving him some sort of explanation. He would want to confront Rathe, then leave the island, which they couldn't do. She knew Rathe wasn't bluffing about taking them to court; he wasn't the type.

It was going to be hard to stay on Andros, with Rathe, for three months, but her only alternatives would produce results far worse. She would not give up her hard-earned self-respect *or* her future with Stavros so easily. She covered herself with the towel again and stared into his eyes, watching him as he no doubt had been watching her these past minutes, forcing the emotion from her expression and from her voice.

"I will stay, under protest, but I will stay and work my best for you until the contract time is up. But I want your promise that you won't tell anyone anything about me, and I want you to leave me alone."

"Okay. Your secrets are as safe with me as mine are with you, and I won't touch you again," he promised. "Not because you've ordered it, but because I don't particularly want to—I take my orders from no one but myself now. I like a woman who doesn't control every honest emotion she feels, who doesn't pretend, who is not a hypocrite."

"Like Carmen, I suppose, who follows you around like a—" She stopped speaking and clenched her teeth together. She couldn't afford the luxury of a full-blown argument now.

"At least she's honest about what she is and what she offers. She hasn't sold herself as some pure, untouched bride whose interests lie with her husband's career and her house full of babies."

"You say that as though it were something vile."

"No." A flicker of emotion crossed his face and was gone. "I don't think marriage with a home and family is vile at all. I wanted the same myself once. . . . But it has to be at the right time and it has to involve two people with equally firm commitments and similar values. It is the person who agrees to enter into a relationship like that and knows beforehand that she can't live up to it who is vile." His stare was cold and affected her like a bath of ice water.

"I don't think I know anyone like that." She shook her head, refusing to believe the description could fit her.

"I think you do. I think if you look deeply into yourself you'll find her, and for such a shallow person that should be easy enough. I'd probably be doing Halkias a favor if I told him about you now and saved him finding out for himself later. You'll never change; if it isn't me, it will be some other man."

"You promised," she broke in.

"I know, and it's probably a promise that we'll both live to regret."

CHAPTER SEVEN

LORELEI WAITED UNTIL the sounds of footsteps and voices had gone from the house before putting away the brightly colored clothing Lucy and taken from her suitcase. The outfit was the kind of thing one would wear for an afternoon picnic with friends; and on Andros, as long as Rathe was here, there could never be any relaxing afternoon picnics, nor could she feel among friends since she was, in effect, in the enemy's camp.

She sighed and tried to collect her thoughts: true, she was stuck here, for three months, on an island with a man who hated her, but moping around her room wasn't going to make her feel better, and it would not help her get through the mountain of uncatalogued salvage next door. And as soon as she finished the work in there, she could leave, putting the entire unbearable episode behind her. With that motivating thought in mind, she changed into a pair of grubbies and set out to tackle the artifact room.

She remembered it to be a jumble of bits and pieces and in need of a cleaning, but she hadn't known how dirty it really was, or in how much of a disorganized jumble. Masses of unidentifiable salvage were thrown here, tossed there—nothing labeled, nothing sorted, heaped mostly in piles of assorted sizes, with only the most obviously valuable things sitting on grimy shelves. The floors were dull too, the once-polished bare wood covered with layer upon layer of dirt, especially in the corners; and the walls and the shelves against them were in equally poor condition. The room's one window was large and would let in more than enough light once the drapes were drawn open and the windows cleaned, but that, in itself, looked like it could take all day. The red velvet draperies might once have been beautiful, but age and dust and sunshine had decayed the fabric until they all but came apart in her hands. The connecting draw-strings broken, she swept the curtaining aside, coughing as the dust and cobwebs of years rained down upon her. She ran a finger down the window glass, the panes too filthy to see out of.

"Yuk, I do not *believe* this room," she said aloud. The rest of the house was immaculate, with nary a dust mote brave enough to land within reach of Lucy's worn and often-used feather duster.

"So what gives in here?" She looked about in frustration, at a loss to pick which of the Herculean tasks needed doing first or most. Absolutely everything needed a good bath, so going after water and rags would have to be the first item on the agenda.

She left the door open. She hoped the room would air out between the time it took to locate the cleaning things and come back up, and that Lucy would have some air freshener. But it looked as if she was to be disappointed on that score. The kitchen was as deserted as the living and dining areas. As spick-and-span as the day before, the kitchen today held none of the smells of freshly baked bread that had enticed her into it yesterday. She looked about in consternation. She didn't want to step on Lucy's toes by rummaging in her cupboards and closets, but she did need the cleaning things . . . badly. Perhaps Lucy had only stepped out for a bit to do—she shrugged—whatever it was that women did who spent their time running a well-ordered home, but just as likely she had gone with the others to see what secrets the little boat in the coral hole held, and she could be gone for hours.

"Can I help you find something?"

Lorelei turned at the sound of the softly spoken question. It was Sarah. The girl was so quiet she had practically forgotten her existence.

"Well, yes, maybe you can. I'm supposed to begin cataloguing the salvage upstairs, but things are a bit on the dirty side and I need to do some cleaning first before I can begin. Would your mom mind if I borrowed a bucket and some rags?"

Sarah answered apprehensively. "I know it's in an awful mess, but Miss Alvarada made it very clear that I wasn't to clean it."

"I wasn't expecting help. I'm sure you have other things to do," Lorelei hastened to assure her. "But just out of curiosity, why didn't she want you to clean it?"

The girl looked down at the floor in embarrassment. "She was afraid I'd damage something valuable out of...ignorance, so she said that I couldn't clean anything until a professional came to move things out of harm's way."

It was obviously a direct quote, and no mistaking who "harm" was supposed to personify. No wonder Ed called Carmen Alvarada the "she-shark," if this was an example of the treatment given his sister.

"Her professional is here now," Lorelei commented dryly. "But some initial cleaning has got to be done before I can even find the artifacts to move them, let alone catalogue them. They are buried, at present, in gook."

The limpid blue eyes looked uncertain, no doubt not believing her bad fortune at having to contend with two fussy females, each with opposing points of view.

"You don't have to help me," Lorelei repeated, trying to reassure the girl. "I won't mention you were involved at all. I just need the cleaning supplies." It was terrible how cowed the girl was. She wondered how much of it had to do with the she-shark and how much with natural shyness, as she watched Sarah pull a bucket from under the sink and fill it with a wide assortment of cloths, window cleaners, grease cutters, detergents and oils, waxes, polishes, and newspapers. Lorelei was staggered by the variety of items.

"Do you think I have everything I need?"

Sarah missed the mild sarcasm and looked critically through the conglomeration. "Almost," she said, adding a bottle of disinfectant floor cleaner and a mop. "Now I think you do."

"Ye gods," Lorelei muttered under her breath and took the heavy bucket. She wouldn't know what to do with half of it, of course, but she could hardly refuse it after having to virtually coerce Sarah to give it to her. Better to stick with detergent and water and let the rest be.

She hoisted the heavy bucket and lugged it back upstairs, managed to fill it with hot water from the bathroom tap, and set it down in the middle of the artifact room floor, but beyond that, she didn't know where to begin. Moreover, cleaning was not one of her favorite things to do.

The floor, she thought, start with the floor and work up. She rolled up her pants and started to work with the mop, but it took only a few minutes to realize that either her detergent was too mild or her elbow grease too ineffectual. The floor wasn't getting much cleaner, and she looked at it dismally, swishing the muddy water in circles. At this rate, her patience would be worn out before her energy, which she was sure would be long gone before the morning was out as well.

"What are you doing?" Sarah's soft, curious question caught her by surprise and she sat back in the water on the floor, blinking at the scrub brush and pail in Sarah's hand. Not more cleaning things! She couldn't cope with what she already had.

"I'm cleaning?" Lorelei ventured.

Sarah wrinkled her nose at the mess and shook her fair-haired head negatively, trying without success to smother giggles. "I'm afraid you're not doing too good a job of it. Did you sweep first?"

"No." So that's what she forgot.

"And the grease cutter, did you add enough?"

Lorelei eyed the unopened bottle still sitting in the bucket.

"Do you want some help?"

It was Lorelei's turn to look uncertain. "Look, I don't want to get you in trouble with the boss or his lady friend, so—"

"Do you mean Rathe? Oh, he's never angry with me. He's a very nice person. It's only Carmen who isn't and I may as well help you. I'll get blamed for it anyway," she responded matter-of-factly.

That was a topic best explored later when the room looked more conducive to friendly conversation. For now it looked like World War III and lacked any of the amenities needed to make it a comfortable place to talk...or work in. And before she forgot—

"Sarah, were there any pieces of furniture in here originally? I'm going to need a large desk to work at and a table for sorting; some lights are a must and a couch would be nice. I thought there might be extra furniture stored somewhere."

"You don't need to do that," Sarah answered quickly. "With the money Rathe has made already, I'm sure he would be more than glad to buy you anything you need."

"No," Lorelei interrupted with finality. Obviously Rathe had pulled the wool over some people's eyes when it came to his real personality, but not over hers, and she had no intention of further obligating herself to him. "I don't want to ask him for anything."

If Sarah thought this a strange attitude for an employee to take with an employer, she didn't hint at it. "You're probably right; it would only give Carmen reason to believe Rathe is paying you special attention. Take it from one who knows, that's a situation you want to avoid." She thought for a minute. "There are a few old pieces up in the attic that opens up off my parents' room. I'm sure no one would object if you used anything there."

Upon reaching the cramped attic, Lorelei could well see why. Every bit of the badly stacked furniture was old, some evidently valuable and antique, some just old, candidates for a yard sale, with layers of dust and portions of their fabric and wood crumbling away. Most of the practical pieces were on the bottom, their heavy, well-constructed bodies used to hold the weight of the rest.

With one eye open for spiders, she hoisted several rickety chairs to one side, revealing what appeared to be a massive walnut desk. She brushed its surface free of dirt. It would do nicely if she could get it out, but blocking its way was a couch, too old and musty-smelling to be considered, and some chairs also, too obscured by boxes to tell whether they would be useful. She perched on the arm of the couch, mindful not to sit on the mice droppings and mold, to formulate her plan of attack. She went over the mental list of furniture she needed.

It was a full two hours later before she managed to get all of the furniture down, including the huge desk, something she had thought to be impossible without crying for help. Rathe was right—she had a stubborn streak where he was concerned and she was determined that if anything needed doing, she would do it herself. She would not need Rathe Drummond . . . for anything. She'd proven that, if only in a small way, this morning, and it gave her a smug sense of satisfaction.

She wiped her grimy hands on her pants and checked the luminous dial of her watch. It was past one; better check on Sarah and see if she had at least made a dent in the cleaning.

The sight that greeted her eyes was astounding. Sarah had managed, somehow, miraculously, to make a great deal more than a dent. The musty, falling-apart drapes had been removed altogether, the dust and cobwebs gone, and the squeaky clean windows were open, allowing sunlight to flood the room and a breeze to replace the dank atmosphere with the aroma of flowers and fresh air, mingling with the smell of Sarah's industrious use of beeswax and lemon cleaners. The artifacts had been placed, carefully, all to one side of the freshly washed and well-waxed floor, and the hardwood shelving that lined the walls had been oiled and polished to a rich, satiny sheen.

The room had been transformed, in the space of two hours, from a virtual dump to a cared-for workplace. The girl was a genie; there was no other explanation.

"I can't believe it. You, Sarah Yates, are positively amazing."

Sarah beamed under the praise. "I was very careful not to damage anything. I didn't think *you'd* mind if I handled things, just to clean under them, you know."

It was a beginning, Lorelei thought. At least the teen-ager trusted her to react more sensibly than Carmen. She dropped a grateful arm over Sarah's shoulders.

"If the surf and the coral and the storms haven't been able to destroy this stuff in a couple of hundred years, I sincerely doubt you would do anything, by accident, to harm it. Actually, I am very grateful for all the help you've given me and I hope to be able to persuade you to do more in the next few days, something more inter-esting than cleaning floors, I hope, but let's talk about it over lunch, shall we? I'm starved."

Sarah proved herself to be as efficient in the kitchen as she had been upstairs and Lorelei couldn't resist saying so over the array of hastily prepared meat and cheese hors d'oeuvres and the tray of sweets.

"I'm green with envy," she said, her mouth full of cheese crumbles.

"If you're not careful, you're going to be wet with tea." Sarah tilted Lorelei's cup upright again.

"Sorry about that." The tea was a spicy, exotic variety

that stimulated her sense of taste as well as her sense of smell, and she wanted to savor it, not spill it. She set the cup down.

"Do you realize that you've whipped up enough food here to feed a small army . . . or your brother . . . whichever comes first?"

Sarah smiled. "So you've noticed that about him already, have you?"

Lorelei nodded humorously. "Yes. The first day when he carried off an entire plate of your mother's scones from under my nose."

Sarah groaned good-naturedly. "That's another of the disadvantages in living here, so far from Nassau and civilization, especially for Ed. He has no manners whatsoever."

"It is beautiful here, though. I'm sure, under the right conditions, it could be like living in paradise, a permanent vacation land."

"I suppose." Sarah was less than enthusiastic. "But people never take vacations anywhere near their homes, do they? Besides, Andros has its drawbacks." She laughed knowingly at Lorelei. "Like our few wild boars. There was a strange old Englishman who loved hunting. He owned this place long years ago and imported the boars. Or so it's said."

Lorelei rolled her eyes heavenward, then took a healthy bite from a homemade confection. "This, Sarah, my friend, this is a skill that my poor, underfed father would give a lot for me to learn. It's something I won't be able to do for Stavros right away, maybe never, unless I get some expert coaching. I don't seem to have the talent."

"I can't believe that; it isn't hard."

"Oh, no? Let me clue you in. I am hopeless in a house—plants die on me, turn brown and shrivel up; I am a simple cook, to put it generously, and I'm as likely to cook with the furniture oil and rub corn oil on my chairs. I assure you, I am hopeless."

"Stavros—I mean, Mr. Halkias,—must love you for other things then," Sarah volunteered, her blue eyes, no longer as washed-out looking as they had been that morning, meeting Lorelei's green ones.

"Please, he would prefer Stavros. When someone says Mr. Halkias, he looks around for his father. And, yes, he must see something else in me besides my home-making skills, but he's the kind of man who would like a nice home with dinner waiting on the table when he gets home, and a wife waiting at the door and all that. He's really very old-fashioned."

"There's hope for me, then, after all. If there's one man around like that, there must be more, right?"

She stood to clear the table, her every movement graceful, yet controlled and efficient. It was too bad she had such a low opinion of herself.

"It's not that I'm lazy and want a man to support me. It's just that if I were to choose a career, it would include all those things that a homemaker does. I love sewing and baking and menu planning and, well, I've thought of doing housekeeping, like mother, to make my living, but I want children too, and I don't want to leave them so I can go and care for someone else's house. I want my own children in my own home, a husband to share it with, a career there..." She blushed. "Mother says what I want is to have my cake and eat it too."

"I don't think so," Lorelei disagreed. "I think most women want those things at one time or another."

"Do you?"

Lorelei picked up her cup and joined Sarah at the sink. "Do I what?"

"Want those things?"

The question was too nearly the same as the one Rathe had asked her this morning, too nearly what she had asked herself ever since seeing Stavros's ring on her finger, realizing she had agreed to the engagement... with reservations known only to herself. She plunged her hands into the dishwater.

"What I really want for now is to get these dishes out of the way and get to work upstairs before the boss shows up and complains that we've been loafing."

"He'd have good reason to complain, wouldn't he?"

Both Sarah and Lorelei turned around simultaneously, the color draining from the younger woman's cheeks. Carmen Alvarada leaned indolently against the kitchen door frame, her bikini-clad body tanned and sleek.

Carmen's dark eyes blazed with anger. "We've been awaiting lunch for almost two hours while you two have been having a tea party. It must be nice to have so much free time on your hands."

"I usually do get them lunch..." Sarah stuttered.

"We've hardly been loafing; our... free time... has been spent working." Lorelei folded her hands and cocked her head toward the draining dishes.

"I'm glad to hear it, but don't you think your time would be better spent upstairs, or do you feel more adequate as a maid?"

Sarah sputtered again without saying anything coherent, trying to placate and explain at the same time, and accomplishing neither goal. Lorelei placed a restraining and, she hoped, calming hand on her arm.

"Why Miss Alvarada, what a thing to say," she responded with a put-on naiveté. "I am much more than capable, much more than adequate at everything I do, but just now, I was helping Sarah with the dishes. I will be needing her help in the next few hours so I thought it would only be fair to give a hand with her work." She took the dish towel from Sarah's startled hands and threw it to Carmen. "But since you're in such a hurry to have us get back to work, I know you won't mind finishing up here for us." She flashed an innocent smile to the smoldering Carmen. "Oh, by the way, Rathe has given me carte blanche with anything I happen to need, and it looks like I'll be needing Sarah for the next few days, perhaps longer, so you all might have to brown bag it for lunch from now on."

Leaving Carmen to recover from the shock, which she prayed would take some time, Lorelei took Sarah in tow and beat a hasty and somewhat undignified retreat upstairs while escape was still possible. They closed the door behind them and burst into peals of laughter, Sarah more from suppressed hysteria than mirth.

"I've never seen her so . . . so . . . so flabbergasted."

Clearly Lorelei had made a friend for life. "Is she always like that?"

"Always," Sarah said regretfully. "Thankfully, it doesn't change the way Rathe treats me."

"What kind of a relationship *do* they have?" She was honestly curious. Carmen seemed so unpleasant that she wondered if the woman got along with anyone.

Sarah shrugged. "Mother says she has his ear; Ed says she has a great deal more than that, but I really don't know. Carmen has said a couple of times that when this job is over, they'll be getting married. Rathe doesn't play favorites though. Even if he's going to marry her, which he's never said, he wouldn't show favoritism. He's too fair."

"Then he won't mind that you're going to help me."

"No, especially when he sees all we've done. There's no room for complaints. Still, it is too bad it won't stay this way."

"Won't stay this way? Why won't it?"

"The same reason it got in that shape in the first place—the artifacts. They bring whatever they happen to find for the day and drop it in here, usually late in the afternoon. They're dirty and gunky and full of sand, which gets all over everything. I finally gave up trying to make sense out of the chaos. As soon as I would try to put things in some sort of order, someone would come along and drop something uncleaned and unrelated into a pile I had all figured out."

Lorelei's face took on a familiar determined look. "Not that I'm criticizing you, Sarah, but things are going to be different now that I'm in charge of this room." She looked guilty. "I feel bad about that, taking over your job. I hope you don't mind. We could share the responsibility."

"No thanks." Her answer was emphatic. "You can have it all—the sand, the books, the she-shark, everything. I will help you, if you weren't just feeding Carmen a line, but I'll really be much happier in the background, only . . ." she faltered. "I'm not sure where you want me to begin."

"Okay." Lorelei looked around the room. "There are a number of things I'll be wanting your help with, but just this minute I was thinking of using the both of us as pack mules for the furniture. Are you game?"

It seemed she was, and with two extra hands the furniture was soon in place.

"What now, boss?" Sarah had an inexhaustible supply of energy.

"We have to get these things cleaned up." Lorelei fingered the coral lamp base. "And I'd like to make a start at some rough cataloguing today. I see you've already done some of it." She pointed to a neatly stacked grouping of breakables "Ceramics, pottery, glassware here; all the gold there." She indicated a shelf that had been cleaned and its costly occupants carefully replaced. By its side lay an unrecognizable pile of metal objects which she squinted at speculatively.

"I see you have silver here, copper . . . but what else? What have you actually catalogued and how is it divided? Have you cross-referenced any of it?" She picked up a note pad and pen.

"Cross-referenced?" Sarah asked, bewildered by the unfamiliar idea. "How?"

Lorelei shrugged. "Oh, I don't know . . . like a list of all the silver items which might include jewelry, coins, containers, instruments. . . . A list of all the jewelry that might include silver, copper, gold, gems . . . you know."

"That was the basic problem, I think. I don't know.

I haven't done much at all. Even Carmen did the gold shelf; anything else was beneath her." She was ashamed. "I shouldn't have said that. She's interested in it all, and she's professional. It's just that she makes it very clear that I'm not." She added a warning: "I hope you are. She can make life purely miserable for us laymen."

Lorelei hoped so, too, and worked frantically for the next couple of hours, painstakingly separating the items into roughly similar groups, setting up cleaning pans and drying trays, and opening a virtual library of books with illustrated pictures and pages of descriptions to help in the identification process, all while Sarah industriously worked around her, unobtrusively cleaning the furniture and picking up after her. They were a good team, working together silently and productively. At last everything in the room was stacked in groupings that Lorelei could understand and work with, rough groupings to be sure and not the final ones she would have them labeled under, but enough to show Rathe, were he to ask, that she had been doing her best to live up to his conditions. Sarah sank back onto the love seat for a well-deserved break, pouring herself and Lorelei a cup of coffee from the coffee maker she'd managed to liberate from the kitchen sometime earlier.

"I can't believe we've done it," she said, wiping at a smudge on her forehead.

"We haven't." Lorelei sipped her coffee slowly, allowing the warm liquid to relax her strained muscles, slow her frantic pace. "We've barely scratched the surface, but it is a start."

"The problem will be in keeping it this way."

As if on cue, the door opened, admitting Stavros, Ed, Carmen, and finally Rathe, each laden with a few pieces of silt- and coral-encrusted material.

"No, you don't...don't put that down." Lorelei jumped up from her comfortable position on the couch and halted the human assembly line that was intent upon ruining the sorting and cleaning process of the last few hours. She pointed to the long table, just inside the door, covered with several layers of soft, cushioning terry cloth.

"Put it all here, gently please, and try not to slop anything on the floor. I'll clean it and sort it all out tomorrow."

Rathe was the first to comment on what must admittedly look, to someone not intimately involved in its careful sorting, to be a terrible jumble.

"We're sorting everything to be cleaned, identified, catalogued, numbered, and put away so it can be easily found again." Lorelei smiled sweetly. It was an art she'd become quite accomplished at while in the tour business, to smile sweetly and explain calmly when all hell threatened to break loose. It sometimes averted trouble, but not this time. Carmen deposited her load of what appeared to be chain on the floor, despite Lorelei's scowl.

"And I thought Sarah was inept," she hissed. "What did you do, stir it up? Oh, I can see that you cleaned the floor, but that's not *your* job, is it? Your job was to put things in order here, and I can't see any order or system to any of this."

Lorelei knew without having to turn around that Sarah felt like sinking into the woodwork. It wasn't her fault if she had neither the training nor the inclination to complete the job. Lorelei assumed a casual stance, but her feelings were anything but casual.

"That's why *I'm* in charge here . . ." *And not you,* she added silently. "I *can* see the organization quite clearly, and I'm sure if Sarah had been given a little more cooperation, she would have managed nicely with her system as well. She's been invaluable today."

"Her ways—" Carmen began.

"Are not as strict as mine are," Lorelei finished firmly. "I require that things be put where I ask." She picked the offending pile of dirty chain up and placed it on the table with the other offerings of the day. "And I need peace and quiet in which to work, so . . ." She waved her hands toward the door expressively, the saccharine smile still in place. Stavros winked as he exited, having seen similar performances before on board ship when an occasional tourist became unruly.

Rathe, who ignored her mandate, remained. With his hands clasped behind his back he stepped around the heaps of artifacts. Long seconds passed, and when he spoke it was with a faint touch of humor.

"Good work, Captain Bligh. However, as your commanding officer I do hope you'll allow me the privilege of supervising your domain every now and again."

Lorelei mentally smoothed her ruffled feathers and poured him a cup of coffee, which he took, without a word, a leaf of laurel between them. She broke the silence.

"Did you find out what was in the little boat Taylor found?"

He nodded. "Yes, in part. The boat looks to be from the ship. It's definitely from the same period of time. The box that Taylor saw is beautiful, but over the centuries it has become attached to the surrounding coral formations, as has the boat. It took all day to get part of the boat out and it may take much longer to get at the chest. I don't want to ruin it simply to get at whatever may be inside." He spoke defensively as if he expected an argument, had maybe gotten one from someone else earlier.

"I agree. To willfully destroy a piece of history that has withstood so much from Mother Nature would be sacrilegious somehow. To ruin the box out of impatience, simply to find out a mere few days sooner what has already waited hundreds of years..." She shook her head. She knew people who would do it, but she was not one of them.

He eyed her curiously. "Why didn't you come out with us today then?"

She supposed she could tell him it was because she hadn't been all that interested, but her statements just now proved otherwise; nor could she tell him she had not been feeling up to it. An hour of lounging on the sand or on a boat would have been easy after the amazonian workload she and Sarah had put themselves through today. She had to tell him something, but there were just so many reasons.

"Partly because I wanted to give you the time to get to know Stavros without me being around. I got the feeling that you might have taken your animosity for me out on him too. You didn't, did you?"

A muscle tightened in his jaw. "I have a great deal of respect for your fiancé. He is very competent . . . and a hard man not to like." The compliment was grudging. She knew that despite his desire to eliminate tension from among his crew, he would have almost preferred to dislike Stavros Halkias, and she noticed that he no longer referred to him as Halkias, but by his Christian name.

"I'm glad you approve of him."

He brushed the compliment aside. "I know how to handle my emotions and act with impartiality when the situation demands it, which is more than I can say for you."

She was caught off guard, unprepared for the attack.

"What on earth are you talking about? I haven't seen you all day."

"I wasn't referring to myself, but to Carmen. She said that you were intentionally rude to her today." He held up a hand to stop her look of outrage. "While you are here, working for me, I fully intend to treat you as anyone else, no special favors or handicaps. It's the only way this can work, if we both forget about our past associations. I do not take one crew member's word over another's without additional proof. I intended to wait until later to speak with you, but after what I've just witnessed, there's no need. You intentionally tried to make her look bad in front of everyone else and you know it. I want it stopped."

She *had* singled Carmen out for a few scathing remarks, but only because no one else would, and that she-shark deserved them! There was no deeper motivation than that.

"All right, so I was rude this afternoon, but Sarah and I worked all morning on this room and she had the nerve to say we were loafing and I *knew* that you'd never believe me..."

"Do you think I'm blind, Lorelei?" he demanded. "Of course I can see that you've been working. I have eyes in my head, woman! I do accuse you of riding roughshod over other people's feelings. It's a trait that goes back a long time with you and I have just seen that you haven't mellowed one bit with age. The poor woman was all but in tears when she came back this afternoon, and I shouldn't wonder if she's in the same state now. She's the best and only photographer I have, Lorelei, and I don't want you to browbeat her. How was she, or any of us for that matter, to know about your new rules... as if you had a right to make new rules without consulting me first. You're nothing but a spoiled prima donna who's had her own way far too long; you're a termagant, Lorelei."

Lorelei stared back at him aghast. Carmen in tears? Crocodile tears, she was sure. Carmen the helpless victim of a termagant? She wasn't entirely certain what that was, but she was aware of the definition of a spoiled prima donna, and she didn't like that. How could he possibly believe that, unless Lucy and Sarah's assumptions were correct and he really was in love with Carmen. Only a man in love could see that woman through such rose-colored spectacles!

"I think you should apologize." His opinion was more in the nature of an order than a request, from the sound of it.

"I will not." Her lips pursed together willfully. Never! Nothing could force her to apologize to that she-shark.

"Haven't you changed at all in the past six years, Lorelei?" he asked disgustedly. "I was prepared to give you the benefit of the doubt..."

Sure you were, she thought cynically. She threw an accusingly disbelieving glare at him.

"But I can see that you are every bit as stubborn, as selfish, and as unfeeling as you always were."

She turned her back on him, prepared to leave the room before she exploded and got herself into worse trouble, but he was not prepared to allow her to go and blocked her exit.

"You don't walk out on me. You may be able to wind every other red-blooded male around your little finger, and you may be able to out-domineer other women, but I say you will stop baiting Carmen. She's too valuable to me. I am the lord and master of this little piece of paradise and I will not allow you to forget it, do you hear me?"

She wanted to scream at the unfairness of it all, but the pressure of his hands on her upper arms was painful and, besides, she owed it to Stavros to keep a lid on the boiling caldron of emotion they brought out in each other if she could. She took a deep, cleansing breath and cleared her mind and felt his hold slacken, and as she did so, impulsively she bowed mockingly, very low in his direction, and started to back out the door, her green eyes dancing with mischievous humor.

"I am at your command, O great one. This poor female servant obeys all your wishes."

He swore softly as her hand touched the doorknob, but in the battle of wits, he was as quick-thinking as she.

"I am glad to hear it; you learn fast. That's how I like my woman to be...meek...mild...well-trained. You may leave my presence...for now." And with that he held her chin firmly between his fingers and kissed her mouth, taking sensual pleasure along with his victory.

His woman? Well-trained? Meek? Never! She'd swim back to Nassau first! Her outraged emotions were plainly evident on her none-too-meek face, and it wasn't until after she'd slammed the door that she heard his mocking laughter and realized she'd been caught in her own trap. She glowered at the closed door, sending her thoughts inward. Round 1 went to Rathe, but there were three long months ahead of them, and it promised to be a very interesting match.

CHAPTER EIGHT

LORELEI BRUSHED A sticky strand of hair from her forehead and blew an overheated breath of air onto her sweaty palms. The humidity had gone up drastically with the temperature, resulting in frayed nerves and short tempers even in the most amiable of their small group, and though she didn't particularly relish working inside, at least she was alone. Having to deal with Rathe or Carmen today along with the heat would tax her thin veneer of patience too far.

She put the half-reconstructed piece of china back on her work table and surveyed the room with a critical, yet approving eye. In the month since coming to Andros she had accomplished a great deal, so much in fact that even Rathe had not been able to complain, and Carmen. . . . She grimaced in displeasure at the thought. Carmen had no logical reason for complaint either, but then Carmen seldom behaved with any logic where Lorelei was concerned. And Lorelei, for her part, had ceased trying to live up to whatever impossible standards of perfection Carmen Alvarada expected, doing her utmost to ignore the photographer's constant flow of not-so-subtle verbal abuse.

Mute tolerance of that thorn in her side might prove difficult today though. She frowned indecisively at the second hand on her watch, which with each passing minute brought Carmen's afternoon photography rounds still closer. She drummed her fingernails atop the work

103

table in frustration, there being a good two, perhaps three hours of work left to her yet. She was hot and tired, unreasonably disgruntled with just about everything, and the last thing she wanted to do was listen to that fault-finding committee of one, whose displeasure with her work seemed to increase on a level directly proportionate to Rathe's approval. Not that he was around to voice it very often. Still, she had the feeling that their "Mexican standoff" was his idea and that he was somehow using it to his advantage.

She covered her project with cheesecloth and set the beautifully illustrated books aside for the time being. She badly needed a break, and a swim in the bay suddenly sounded like an exceptionally good idea, more so if Stavros could be persuaded to join her. They had spent very little time together since coming to the island. Her days were devoted to the cleaning, restoring, and cataloguing of the artifacts that were brought up daily; his were spent in and around the wreck or topside with the other divers, and with Sarah, who, though she had proven herself invaluable onboard with the rough processing of the artifacts, was not his fiancé. He must be missing her company as much as she missed his, and she planned to make up for that neglect today.

Dressing hurriedly in a snug-fitting, pale cream bikini, she left the plantation house and skipped lightly over the sandy trail that led to the beach, pulling a bright purple passion flower from its vine and winding it into her hair as she went.

"Stavros!" she called. "Hey, over here!" She cupped her hands to her mouth and shouted over the water toward the boat that contained Stavros and, to her consternation, Carmen as well. She tried to be philosophical; one had to take the bad with the good. She waved to him and broke into a run as he saw her and turned the small boat back to shore.

"What are you doing out here?" Carmen was the first to speak after they'd landed, leaving Stavros to drag the boat up onto the sand alone.

Her nemesis stood a few feet away, a basket of coral-encrusted artifacts under her arm, the perpetual, pouting frown in place on her face. She looked to be in a particularly nasty mood.

Lorelei directed her reply to a wet-suited Stavros instead. "I'm taking the day off."

Refusing to be ignored, Carmen sauntered closer. "Just like that, without permission from anyone?"

"Yep." She swallowed the acid comments with difficulty. Backbiting and bitchiness weren't her style, but Carmen was skating on thin ice. She flopped down onto the sand beside Stavros, who was melting from the heat, if the looks of him could be any judge.

"Whew! That's work. What's up, sweetheart?"

She glanced around at the hovering she-shark, wishing she would go away. She wanted to have a private conversation. "I was hoping you could take a couple of hours off and come swimming with me, or go for a walk, if that's more to your liking." Even as she asked, she had the impression his answer would be negative.

"I wish I could." He hugged her close, dampening her bikini with seawater. "But it's my turn to go down next and when I'm done with that, I tell you, I don't even want to see the water unless it's in a nice cool bath."

"Oh, well, it was just a thought." She understood; work came first. The problem was, work had come first for the past month and she felt no closer bond to Stavros now than she had before coming on their supposed "working holiday," so rarely had she had the chance to spend time with him.

"Tell you what, can I get a rain check?" He hadn't missed her drooping chin. "How about a walk after dinner?"

"I wish I could say the same," Carmen interrupted. "I'll probably still be working then, doing my job and other people's as well, that is, unless you want to take these back with you when you go." She held out the basket expectantly.

"I'm not going back in there today, Carmen." Lorelei

bit her lip to keep from arguing the afternoon away. "I need a break."

With a muttered, "Don't we all?" Carmen left them alone, trudging melodramatically back to the plantation.

"God, it's hot. I wish they made these things with ventilation." Stavros plucked at the skin-tight rubber suit without effect.

"You'd better head back for the water then, before you bake."

He stole a look at the sun. "I should, but I hate to leave you like this. You shouldn't let her get to you, you know."

"Do you think we could do something together before I turn into a piece of history?" Lorelei asked. "You know I haven't had a day off yet."

He stood up and brushed the sand from his hands before extending one of them to her. "I'm way ahead of you. Actually, Carmen's been climbing all over Sarah too. I thought the poor kid was going to jump ship this morning. I was thinking we could all go diving Sunday; get away from it."

"All?" There went her romantic plans for the day. There were times when his hands-off attitude toward any kind of intimate courtship drove her to distraction. She was too liberated to condone a chaperone.

"Sarah, you and me. Do you know that she lives with two of the finest divers I've ever met and they haven't taught her how?" He tutted his disapproval. "We could teach her to dive, you and I, maybe have a picnic later. What do you say?" He squinted out over the water. "Listen, I have to go back out, but we'll talk about the details later, okay?"

"Okay," she responded to thin air as he fairly ran back to the boat and to the cooling water. She watched him grow smaller and finally disappear, blending in with the waves as they hit the reef, and toyed with the idea of going back to work, prodding her conscience to change the answer to a question she had already come to a decision on. She'd earned this day, and if she had to spend it alone, fine. She had learned to enjoy her own company a long time before Stavros came along, and if their engagement wasn't progressing as she'd hoped it would, well, today wasn't crucial. She could always make time for him later, if she wanted to.

The sand was warm, and fine white grains of it sifted through her toes as she walked away from the plantation's problems. The feeling was delicious and long overdue. She strolled closer to the water where the sand was firmer, allowing the almost bathwater-warm waves to caress her feet, twirling gracefully around, drinking in the beauty of the island that she had only seen so far from the window in her room, as if in a picture. The panorama of sand, sea, and sky was like a painting, three-dimensional, unbroken by the geometric lines of civilization's buildings, its serenity unmarred by anything except the cries of the seabirds.

She skipped a seashell over the water, watching as it came tumbling in and was drawn out again. The sun was still hot, but she broke into a run anyway, allowing her stiff muscles the luxury of unrestrained movement until a twinge in the calves of her legs and the sweat accumulating on her brow forced her to stop and reminded her that she had not yet taken her intended swim. The turquoise water was as cool and as clear as glass and far from the hustle and bustle of the plantation at this spot.

She looked around, tempted. Wouldn't it be nice to swim as nature intended, without the pale cream bikini that attracted sand like a magnet and that only interfered with an overall tan? The thought was hardly formed before her towel found its way to the sand, her bikini to the towel, and she to the water.

She dove dolphinlike, under and up, back and forth, chasing a small fish that nibbled at her toes, diving for the sea grass that tickled her legs, until she had expended her nervous energy. She paddled in to shore until she could stand, walking unconsciously from the water where foamy waves caressed her thighs, until her eyes found the towel, the bikini—and the man who sat beside them, silently puffing his pipe. There was no way for her to turn back. It was too late, and in any case, she would have to come out some time for her clothes. Better to brazen it out now than to cower in the shallows until he decided to leave, which he probably wouldn't, just to avoid causing her embarrassment.

He called to her. "You look like the mythical Venus rising out of the water."

She supposed she should be flattered, but she wasn't. The nerve of the man! "What are you doing here?"

His eyes traveled over her body, all ivory pale without recent exposure to the sun, assessing her long, slim legs, firm stomach, and up-tilted breasts provocatively, knowing, and not caring at all, that it made her uncomfortable.

She made a grab for the towel, gritting her teeth as a fine film of beach sand covered her skin. "Rathe, I asked you a question," she reminded him. "I want to know what you're doing out here—spying on me?"

He looked unperturbed. "It was my turn up, my last dive for the day. Carmen said you had taken the afternoon off, so I came to find you."

Simple enough. She suppressed the desire to rant and rail at his girlfriend's telling tales. He wouldn't appreciate it and would only accuse her of having it in for the woman. She slapped one hand against her towel-covered thigh in exasperation.

"How did you find me? All I wanted was the afternoon off."

He cocked one eyebrow and tapped the ash from his pipe. "Me too. I have no intention of dragging you kicking and screaming back to the house. Stavros thought you might want company, but I can see Carmen was right. In your present frame of mind . . ."

Carmen again. She was beginning to hate the name, though Rathe seemed sincere. "I'm sorry." She held out a hand in apology. "It isn't the people I needed to get away from, but the work. I enjoy it very much most of the time." She paused, not certain he would understand.

"But too much of a good thing is still too much."

"Uh-huh." She nodded. "I've started to talk to myself, and in seventeenth-century Spanish at that."

"And even I'm preferable to that."

A smile tugged at the corners of her mouth. The swim and the run had been good for her and she could hardly hold it against him that he caught her skinny dipping. It had been her idea. Why shouldn't she enjoy his company for the day? "We'll have to see about that."

"Fair enough. What do you want to do for the rest of the afternoon?"

"I don't know." She thought a minute. "It's been so long since I've had any free time that I've totally forgotten how to use it."

He tossed a shellful of sand at her, covering her bare feet. "I refuse to believe that I'm such a slave driver."

"No," she admitted. "But you work so hard yourself that it makes the rest of us feel guilty when we don't."

"I find it hard to pace myself."

She knew that, and had known it ever since that long-ago summer. There was an air of excitement about him even when he sat perfectly still, only in part explained by what he had to say. It *was* a quality find and he had a right to be excited, yet the energy, the dynamics came from within. He had always had the quality of being more vitally alive than anyone else. It had drawn her to him in the beginning and the potency of the attraction had not faded with time. She pulled the toweling tighter across her taut breasts.

"I'd like to do some exploring today, so, if you'll turn your head I'll get dressed."

He closed his eyes instead, his expression unreadable as she dropped the covering, her body tingling with the forbidden excitement. She shook the feeling off and spoke to him to relieve the mounting tension.

"Are you going back to the plantation?"

"Eventually," he replied dryly. "I live there. For now I think I'll come explore with you...in case you run into any more wild boar."

"If I do—" she laughed, "—I think I'll cook and eat him right there on the spot. I missed lunch and suddenly I'm famished."

"Do you want to go back?"

Why did she have the feeling he was asking her more than the obvious?

"No. Not yet." She finished dressing quickly.

He stood up and fell in beside her as she walked, away from the plantation, his gait casual, the sand clinging to his bare feet and to the denims that were tightly fitted to his lean hips.

"Good." He seemed genuinely pleased. "We can find something to eat later—berries...raw fish...that is, unless you've grown soft with all the high-society pampering Stavros has gotten you used to."

"I've eaten raw fish; it wouldn't be the first time." She took a walk down memory lane. They had eaten raw clams once for breakfast.

"But in how many years?" he called back the rhetorical question.

The trail he chose to lead her along paralleled the water, but the beach, as such, all but disappeared, scraggly pines almost meeting the water's edge, the sand sucked away by the tides, the ground littered with sharp, dark rocks that hurt her feet and looked like they had been ripped from the jagged cliffs that loomed above.

"Ow!" she cried out in pain. "Rathe, where are you taking me and how much farther are we going? And while we're on the subject, who put you in charge of this expedition?" Most likely he had just taken command in that brash, presumptuous way of his. She didn't remember him asking if he could drag her over the bed of nails she felt herself to be walking on. He was a most inconsiderate man.

"Patience, woman. Don't you believe in the old saying, all good things come to those who wait?"

"I'm not waiting anywhere," she reminded him. "I'm being dragged and the only thing that's going to come to me is sore feet. Rathe, I'm barefoot!" She stumbled over a stone and hopped along behind him in a curious high-stepping march, nursing a bruised toe along with her irritation.

"We're almost there," he called back to her and turned into the surf to go around a large outcropping of rock.

"If you're leaving home, you're headed in a very bad direction."

The waves drowned out her shouting as the water crashed against the protruding rocks, and she was glad when he finally turned back to shore, following the head-high wall of stone that separated them from the way they had come. The mountains came all the way down to the sea here on either side of them—sharp, steep boulders hiding their tiny alcove from eyes on both sides, looking a little like a cookie with a giant bite missing from its middle. Mother Nature had hewn a semicircle in the rocky mountain face, leaving fine sand in its place and a gaping hole going back into the mountainside farther than she could see.

"A cave?" She was filled with curiosity.

"More than a cave, much more. Come on, I'll show you." He reached back to put an arm about her shoulders, stopping midway as she stepped back. "You'll be sorry when the Lusca gets you, but don't say I didn't offer my protection."

She stopped short, doubtful, not quite as curious about the cave as before. A . . . what did he call it? She took a few tentative steps forward, prepared to retreat fast if something moved from within the recesses of the darkened maw. The cavern floor was entirely sand, and as far as she could see there were no animal footprints. The sea air had left a fresh, sweet smell inside and an atmosphere that was surprisingly dry. She could detect no animal odor, nor indeed any sign that the cave had an occupant either animal or human.

"A Lusca?" she ventured. "Don't tell me there's something more unfriendly here on Andros than the boar . . . or you." She raised an eyebrow to him meaningfully.

"Ah, but that's not true. I'm not unfriendly, sweet siren; you're unapproachable."

"I am not a siren, nor am I unapproachable," she added. "But how would you know? I haven't noticed you coming anywhere near me lately."

"So you did notice." His reply was smug. "Reverse psychology works after all. I wondered how long it would take you to climb down from your ivory tower if I wasn't pounding on the door night and day, demanding that you come out."

His perception was unsettling; it was also stimulating. She played along with his game. "How do you know the shoe isn't on the other foot, that I might not have been manipulating you unawares?"

"How so?" He leaned against the rocks, his hands thrust in the front pockets of his denims.

"I could have wondered how long it would take you to come to me if I secluded myself in the ivory tower." She grinned with the victory. "And if I recall corectly, you followed me today, not the reverse."

"Maybe now you'll believe me when I say you're a siren."

She balled the wet towel up and threw it at him. "Touché! I can't win with you, can I?"

"I didn't know you wanted to." He snapped her legs with the towel which she grabbed before it could come into contact with her skin, and pulled it from his hands.

"Rathe, why did you follow me today, honestly?"

"Maybe I remembered how much I used to enjoy your company. Maybe I just wanted to show you the Lusca. Are you coming?"

He walked unhesitantly into the mouth of the cavern, leaving her no choice but to follow him or stay behind alone, as she would. She followed, hunching over as the ceiling height lowered, and caught up with him.

"What is it?"

"What is what?"

"The Lusca. Rathe, don't be difficult. What is it?"

The walls narrowed and the ceiling lowered further until they were almost on their knees before it finally turned into another passageway and opened up into a larger, perhaps fifteen-by-twenty, stone room, tall enough to stand and move about in. Rathe chose to sit though, and kneeling down onto the sandy floor, motioned for her to do the same. He whispered in her ear.

"We're in the lair of the Lusca; half dragon, half octopus. He lives in the island caves and eats anyone who comes close enough . . . raw."

"And I almost believed you. What a terrible imagination you've got."

"Not my imagination," he corrected. "It's a bona fide legend started by the very first people to use these caves."

"Do you mean we're not the first people to crawl into this delightful place?" She mocked the bare stone walls, primeval in appearance.

"Not even the second. The outer rooms used to be quite popular. Not everyone was brave enough to crawl back this far, though."

"Can't say as I blame them, whoever they were."

His voice was soft and it reverberated richly off the walls. "The list of visitors includes some long-gone Seminole Indians, some longer-gone pirates, perhaps a stranded ship's crew, and now us."

He plumped a pile of sand into a more comfortable backrest and leaned onto it. "Feel honored?"

"I'm not sure." She laughed. "The entrance is open to the sea. If there's no Lusca, why weren't there any tenants between the Indians and you?"

"I've made improvements. It wasn't always like you see it. I stumbled onto it, or, more accurately, into it several years ago. The entrance had been covered by a landslide and in climbing over the rocks, I slipped through a hole. I moved the rocks and crawled in."

"Adventurous sort, aren't you?" She tilted her head to get a better view of the ceiling, her apprehensive scrutiny amusing him.

"It happened a long time ago from the look of things."

"Was it worth the discovery? Did you find anything of value?"

"Depends on your definition. There were a few things in the outer room—fishbones, rough tools, spearheads. The Seminoles probably used it as a smoking room for the fish they caught. The ceiling and walls were smoke-blackened. I found something more in this room, something that helped me to finance my own expeditions and eventually to locate the ship." He paused for effect, watching her face, looking to judge her reaction. "I found four solid silver bars with the identifying marks to prove they were from the galleon *Princess*."

She cupped her hands to her cheeks and settled into a more comfortable position. "The *Princess*. Funny, I've been working on her contents for weeks and I didn't even know her name. Tell me about her."

"The woman or the ship? The galleon *Princess* was named after a real Spanish princess whom the son of the galleon's owner hoped to marry. He had gathered gifts for her, and after doing a few minor things for his father was supposed to pay his court to her in Spain. He never made it and now he's down there with his presents and the only princess he ever knew—the galleon."

"How do you know all the details?" He told the story with feeling, as if he knew it by heart, as if he had known that long-ago Spanish boy and shared in his dreams. It was a sentimental side of his personality that was not allowed to govern his own private life. She tossed a wave of hair back and concentrated on what he said.

"I've spent a great many days in Spanish museums looking over all the catalogued and uncatalogued papers, diaries, logs. I've known about the *Princess* for a long time. I had her history, her destination, her manifest, everything but the location of her final resting place, and once I found the cave, I found that. A lucky chance of fate, don't you think?"

"I don't understand."

"There was a rough map of Andros etched onto one of the silver bars and a diagram of where the *Princess* had gone down."

That piqued her curiosity. "So there were survivors?"

"I don't know that for sure." He shrugged. "There might have been. She could have gone down in a storm, there could have been surviving crew; or she could have been set upon, fired upon by pirates—this area was renowned for them—and the ship sunk before her cargo could be fully salvaged, only that which I found in the cave rescued." He held his hands up uncertainly. "In any case, the etching was there and no one came back to claim either the silver or the galleon."

"Maybe they died trying to save the rest of the crew."

"More likely drowned trying to save the rest of the cargo, or died in other battles. A pirate had a very short life span. I doubt they would have tried to save anyone on board unless there were women, and even then it would have depended upon the women."

"What would have happened to them—" she raised an eyebrow, "—eventually?"

"Stout, stern Spanish duennas, thumbs down; demure virgin beauties would have stood a better chance. If they looked like you, an expensive sultan's harem in the desert." He reached to caress her dark hair.

"No, Rathe, I don't think..."

He kissed her lips hungrily, imprisoning both her hands with one of his. "If the pirates had rescued you and brought you to this place, you wouldn't have had to think, that wouldn't have been your purpose, and I don't imagine it would have been all that important if you were willing or not. In fact, it would have lent spice to the taking if you weren't."

She wet her lips self-consciously, aware of the taste he left behind. "And are you playing pirate again, Rathe,

with your buried treasure and your sunken galleon and
your making love to women you don't love?"

He stroked her shoulders, his hands moving downward, the bikini top no deterrent to his searchings, his
fingers causing sensations of excruciating intensity to
well up inside of her. She desperately wanted him to stop
and to go on at the same time, her fingernails digging
into the skin of his arms as his lips replaced his fingers,
his mouth favoring the twin peaks with equal fervor.

"I'm not playing at anything, Lorelei. I'm very
serious. I want you. I've tried not to but, God help me,
I still do."

She held herself stiffly. "You can't have me. I'm not
a shy Spanish virgin willing to be raped by a pirate. This
is the twentieth century. I'm engaged now to another
man and you're my employer, nothing more." Water off
a duck's back, she reflected ruefully. He wasn't listening,
caught up in a whirlpool of violent emotion that threatened to engulf her as well.

"Not a shy virgin," he breathed. "But the pirate who
first loved you didn't have to rape you. I can't believe
you've forgotten."

"That was a long time ago. I have Stavros now."

"I don't think so. I don't think he's made love to you
or done more than give you sweet, brotherly kisses." He
proceeded to show her the opposite of the sweet, brotherly kiss; savage, devouring, anything but brotherly. He
held her captive, but whether by physical strength or
strength of will, she wasn't sure. Her grip on morality,
on her once well-defined set of values was slipping. She
gasped in dismay and wriggled from his grasp.

"You know what they say, behind closed doors. For
all you know, Stavros and I could be very intimate. It's
not your business."

His fingers bit into the flesh of her upper arms. "Even
if I thought that was true, I'd still want you; you've
become a need in my blood, an ache in the rest of me.
I want to make love to you now, before we go back to

the plantation where Stavros, his family, and your father can change your mind, before they fit you into their respectable, safe, conforming mold and destroy that wild, impulsive woman I used to know. She is unique and spirited and so very beautiful. . . . And they will destroy her."

There was no denying that he wanted her, and that she wanted him equally. She could only hope to deny that feeling's physical expression . . . maybe. He lay practically on top of her, his body so close that she could smell the faint aroma of his after-shave mixed with the salty tang of the sea air and that of his own body chemistry. It aroused her without him being aware of it. How much more could he arouse her if he but tried?

She ran her fingers sensuously along his tanned arms, wishing she could touch more, wishing she could touch it all, the places that had no exposure to the sun, caress him with her hands that worked their way around the corded muscles of his back, with her breasts that tingled with the electricity of desire as they brushed against the hair on his chest. An infinitesimally small part of her being wished she could leave while there was still time, but the movements she made beneath him were not movements of escape, and as she felt his response to her, she knew that a decision to go . . . or to stay had to be made now, while rational thought was still possible.

"My beloved pirate . . ." she mouthed the words, sounding like the whisper of a breeze in the cave. How easy it would be to give in to the passion he offered. Yet she had gone that route before, and after the passion there was nothing more for her than the ashes of the aftermath, only pain and the endless, eternal loneliness. She would have to begin the process of forgetting him all over again . . . if he could be forgotten. It was too high a price to pay for a few moments in his arms. She rose from his embrace stiffly.

"I won't do this to Stavros." She wouldn't do it to herself; in reality, Stavros, as selfish as that sounded, hadn't entered into the decision at all.

"So be it." He rolled away from her, not threatening or pleading or arguing with her, though she could sense that he wanted to.

His pain was hers and she bent to touch him. "Rathe, try to understand..."

"I do," he shouted. "Don't make it worse. You've made your decision, so go, now, before...while I still have the presence of mind or the stupidity to allow it."

"But Rathe—"

"*Go!*"

She closed her mind to the desire they shared and left the cave, traversing the beach back to the plantation alone, lest she lose her resolve and go back to him on whatever terms he offered, no matter how temporary she knew they would be.

CHAPTER NINE

SHE WAS STILL shaking by the time she reached the out-
skirts of Rathe's landscaped plantation grounds. There
was a reason she had avoided him for the first four or
five weeks on Andros, a reason that she had been reminded of just a few minutes ago — she *was* so desperately attracted to him, though that was a gross under-
statement of the emotion she felt, that they both obviously
felt. He was attracted to her as well and that feeling
could, if they were to let it get out of control, destroy
the happiness she wanted to have with Stavros and the
future that Carmen Alvarada boldly stated Rathe planned
to have with her. The truism, you can't go home again,
fit her and Rathe to a tee. There was too much distrust,
too many other commitments for their relationship to be
given a second chance. She had to believe the feeling
between them would die when she married Stavros; that
this aching emptiness would be a temporary thing. She
had to.

"Something wrong, Lorelei?" Carmen's harsh, grating
voice reached her ears.

Nothing she could talk about; she frowned. "What are
you doing out here this time of day?" she asked Carmen.
It was late. The sun had set long ago and there wasn't
even a dull orange-red in the sky to indicate the day was
newly gone.

"I'm looking for Rathe," she responded, as if that had
been obvious. "Have you seen him?"

119

"No." She shivered as Carmen resumed her search, much like her nickname's sake, in a single-minded frenzy. What had possessed her to lie about seeing Rathe? Guilt, she answered herself. The fact was, her day with Rathe had been anything but innocent and surely that guilt was written all over her face, for everyone to see, including Stavros, who was engrossed in a checkers game with Sarah when she entered the house.

"Who's winning?" She endeavored to keep her voice light.

"Her," Stavros responded forlornly as Sarah knocked another checker piece off the table. "She's murdering me."

Sarah laughed, a light lilting sound, and reached forward to push a lock of Stavros's unruly hair back out of his eyes. "Only because you're too tired to concentrate."

"You're right about that one."

"Stop it, both of you. You're making me feel guilty about my day out." In more ways than one, Lorelei old girl, she told herself. She ruffled Stavros's hair. "I think I'll go change while Sarah beats you at cutthroat checkers."

"Confidence," Stavros moaned. "Even my fiancée doesn't have confidence in me."

She hurried upstairs and slumped in a confused heap on her bed, chewing a fingernail nervously. This would never do. It would take no special intuition to see something was wrong, drastically wrong with her, and while Stavros was trusting, he was no fool. She jumped as the sound of a knock reached her ears.

"Who is it?" She didn't want to see any more of Rathe this evening.

"The loser at checkers. I've come to collect my consolation prize."

She opened the door to him, winding her arms about his neck. "I don't know if I like that, being a consolation prize."

"Honey, if you're what the loser gets, I'll make it a

point to let someone else win every time." He nuzzled her neck, then moved with her into the room, closing the door behind him.

"I missed you today."

"I missed you too." It was true. If he had come with her, none of the past several hours would have happened. It was what she got for playing hooky when everyone else had to work. She kissed him deeply, searching for the fire in him that had all but consumed her earlier, but he broke off the embrace and held her lightly.

"I *have* been busy lately. Have I been neglecting you?"

"Dreadfully." She teased him lightly. "But now that you're here..." She started to speak but footsteps from outside in the hall prevented it.

"I should have known," he whispered. "This doesn't look good." She still wore the skimpy bikini. "Do you want to get the door, or shall I?"

"Neither of us?" She asked him hopefully.

He threw her a wry grin but opened the door anyway to reveal, much to her secret annoyance, Rathe, still wearing the sandy cut-offs.

"Sorry to interrupt." He didn't look the least bit sorry. "But Taylor just brought up an entirely intact vase that I'll want to have photographed just as soon as Lorelei has gotten it cleaned."

"Intact?" Stavros echoed. "Where is it? I'd like to see it."

She shot Rathe a distrusting look. How like him to interrupt them with something he knew Stavros would want to see right away. He'd probably done it on purpose.

"Taylor has it downstairs, but before you get involved, see if you can locate Carmen, will you? Tell her I want that vase photographed tonight."

"Sure thing Rathe. Do you have any idea where she is?"

"At the site, I'm pretty sure."

"I'll see you later." He kissed her on the cheek and was gone.

She waited until he had closed the door. "I saw Carmen, when I came in, going the other direction, down the beach."

"I know."

Her eyes widened at the implication. "They may never find each other."

"They will," he contradicted. "But the search will buy us the time we need to complete some unfinished business."

"You sent him away on purpose." She'd supposed as much right in the beginning.

"Yes. I won't have you taking him to bed to prove to yourself that you don't want *me* there."

Her breathing quickened at his words. "We can't go on like this." Even he must see it was tearing her apart.

"I'm aware of that. That's why things have to change between us. I should never have let you go today. I was wrong; I can't live with your decision, and I can't continue to sneak around Stavros's back in my home."

"We can't do this. I'm promised to him; I'm engaged to him."

"He doesn't own you, damn it! I don't own you; no one could." He stepped closer to touch her hands, trying to convince without frightening her. "To love me, or not, is your choice, my little mermaid, my sea witch with the emerald eyes. No one should be able to live your life *for* you. I don't ask that. . . . I want to live your life *with* you. Let me, please."

He crushed her to his chest and this time she did not struggle to escape, could not struggle against them both anymore. At the sound of a door opening she tried to pull away, but couldn't. She melted against him, surrendering herself to him.

Lorelei rubbed her tired, gritty-feeling eyes and wondered yet again why she didn't get up and do something. She had dozed, fitfully, since coming to bed a full four hours ago, if the clock on her bedside table was to be believed. She turned the clock entirely around to be sure; the time was 3:00 A.M. Surely she hadn't been lying here awake, wrestling with her problem all that time?

No. For an hour or so after leaving Rathe, she had lain in the bed wide awake, not thinking at all, just listening passively to the movements in the next room. She imagined him in her mind's eye as she heard him get into bed...alone. She heard him, every time he moved, and he tossed and turned a lot. She recalled being awake when he uttered a spiteful oath and left his sleepless bed too, pacing the room next door in short, furious steps. She knew how he felt, had a share in his frustration.

It had taken every ounce of willpower she possessed to leave him in the end. She had allowed her desires free rein until she knew there could be no turning back. In truth, after he carried her through their connecting bathroom to his bed, there would have been no turning back had he not left her for a brief moment, just long enough to allow him to lock the main door, his lithe body fevered with desire, taut, just barely controlled. In that instant, she had fled through the bathroom, her clothes tightly held in her arms, slipping through his fingers, ignoring the entreaties and threats he half whispered through the connecting door, ignoring, as best she could, the way her own body quivered in response to the sound of his voice. What to do now?

She was no closer to an answer now than she had been four hours ago. She threw back the blankets and drew on a robe. She *would* go stark raving mad if she had to think about it any more tonight, and what to do about Rathe was not a decision she intended to make in the state of mind she was in at present.

She tiptoed down the hall to the artifact room and snapped on the overhead light. The vase Taylor had brought up earlier was exquisite, its intrinsic elegance obvious even under the layers of grime. Found in a metal chest, its creamy porcelain base wrapped in layers of

decomposed cloth and sludge, it had withstood the ug-
liness of the storm and the cry of the dying ship and her
crew, the ravages of the coral and the loneliness of the
years. It stood serene, waiting patiently, wanting only
a little cleaning to restore it to its original splendor.

She worked on it ever so carefully, lovingly, engrossed in the restoration process for the better part of
an hour until its transulcent form gleamed pristine and
she could almost smell the heady fragrance of the red
roses painted symmetrically about its middle. She washed
the silt and grime from herself as well and left the prize
where it stood on her work table. She would show it off
tomorrow.

She fell asleep at once upon returning to her room,
the work dispelling the worries in her mind temporarily,
but her slumber was rudely interrupted very early the
next morning as Rathe burst into her room, his expression
black, his entire countenance a picture of uncontrolled
fury. He flung himself on the bed, his knees straddling
her waist.

"Wake up, damn you! How can you sleep after what
you've done?"

She awoke to a shaking and loud voices, and it took
a moment to focus her eyes on her attacker. "What's
wrong?" She tried to sit up but he pushed her back onto
the bed and rose from it himself, trembling in rage.

"Don't lie to me this morning, Lorelei, or so help me
I'll strangle you with my bare hands."

"What did I do? What is the matter . . . Rathe?" Her
eyes echoed her heart's astonishment. "Surely you aren't
still angry about last night?" She had known he was
upset, but this upset? He looked haggard, his face un-
shaven, the carpet of dark stubble and the unkempt hair
making him appear even more fierce.

"Don't give yourself that much credit," he hissed.
"I've been turned down by whores before . . ." He spat
the insult at her. "But they usually agree to a price before
they start work and they don't back out at the last minute.

But that isn't the problem right now and you know it."

She could only guess how much he had heard, but Stavros appeared in the doorway then, followed by Sarah and a strangely smug Carmen.

"What's the trouble, Rathe?" Stavros looked in concern from the two ash-pale faces, each overcome by emotion.

"The vase . . . the vase! It's broken, smashed into a thousand pieces, and she did it!" He pointed accusingly to Lorelei.

If she had been proclaimed a witch she could hardly have been more horrified. "I didn't . . . I wouldn't have." It was unthinkable.

"Shame on you, Rathe Drummond." Drawn by the shouting, Lucy scolded him. "You've frightened the poor child nigh to tears."

"That's a harsh accusation, son," Taylor said as he entered and went to stand by his employer whose hopes and ambitions he shared, but whose quicksilver emotions where the girl was concerned he did not. "It had to have been an accident. The girl has a great love for these things, she'd not willfully destroy anything. I know your disappointment, but what you're saying is not reasonable."

"Reasonable?" He mouthed the word to find its meaning, sweeping from the room with a nightgowned Lorelei and the remainder of the household in his wake.

Lorelei brushed past him and entered the room first, her hands flying to her face in horror as she knelt beside the work table and the atrocity underneath. Tiny, minuscule shards of translucent porcelain lay among what once had been blood-red roses, but the rose shape was unrecognizable and all that remained was the color of blood in the tiny pieces of ceramic that dotted the floor. There was no one piece bigger than a fingernail and she did not doubt that the destruction had been deliberate. Someone had maliciously invaded her sanctuary and desecrated it in the worst possible way. There would be, could be, no way to put the sacrifice together again. She wept silently, not caring that everyone stared at her.

Rathe's tone of voice was grim. "Did you come in here after you left me last night, Lorelei?"

The Spanish Inquisitors must have sounded just like that. "Yes, I couldn't sleep so I came in here to work on the vase, but it was whole when I left it."

"Well, of course it was." Sarah extended a comforting arm to her, throwing Rathe an uncharacteristic look of defiance.

He flipped a photograph of the whole vase to Lorelei. "It's a good thing Carmen was able to get a picture of it then, because it isn't whole now." He snapped out yet another question. "Carmen, what time did you take this picture?"

She looked startled but recovered herself quickly. "Why, I don't quite recall. Everyone was still downstairs, everyone, that is, except you and her." She glanced coldly at Lorelei. "So I guess it must have been about ten."

But that couldn't be; Lorelei frowned, perplexed. The picture showed the vase after it had been cleaned, yet she had not cleaned it until after 3:00 A.M. that morning. She knew it would do no good to protest, however. With her recent complaint of overwork, no one would believe she would quit her bed in the middle of the night to clean the vase.

"It does look intentional," Stavros admitted aloud, confirming everyone's thoughts. "How tight is your security?"

Rathe's eyes narrowed to slits and turned on Lorelei. "I'm sure you all know the answer to that one. I know who destroyed the vase."

"She doesn't have a motive for that," Stavros insisted. "None of us do."

"Her motives are for her to say, it's not my place. But she has them; she's responsible and she's going to pay for it dearly."

He jerked her to her feet before their startled eyes and half dragged her down the hall, oblivious to anyone's protests, especially her own. He thrust her into her room and closed the door.

"Get dressed in water gear. You have exactly one minute."

She was out in just that amount of time, dressed in a one-piece, low-cut red suit. "Am I to leave the island? Where are we going?"

He refused to answer and forced her down the stairs at his side, his fingers biting cruelly into her arm, but they were stopped at the door. She had never seen Stavros angry; even now he was only determined.

"You don't know that she's to blame and I won't allow you to take her from this house."

Rathe's facial muscles tightened to stone and he snarled to her out of the corner of his mouth. "Call him off, woman, or he'll get a rude awakening about you right now."

She couldn't let Stavros defend her. She knew that she alone could resolve this crisis.

"It's all right, Stavros. I'll go wherever he wants to take me. I'm sure I can get it all straightened out."

Stavros remained stubbornly planted against the door.

"Please, Stavros."

In the end he capitulated, albeit reluctantly, watching them as they left the house with a silent, curious contemplation.

"Where are you taking me?"

He shoved her none too gently into the little boat moored at the docks and started its engine. "You're going swimming; you're going to replace what you destroyed if it takes you forever." He drew up beside the larger craft, anchored, she knew, just above the wrecked Spanish galleon. "You're going under with me. Here, put these on."

He handed her a wet suit, air tanks, flippers, and

assorted hardware which she wasted no time in donning, sure that he would drag her below when he was ready, whether she was fully suited-up or not; yet once in the water he did not touch her further, leaving her for the allure of the wreck, the remains of which she could see below them. The wood had long since rotted, replaced by the coral, and it was easy to see why it had lain undiscovered until now. The treasure, all the ship's contents, would have fallen to the sand and coral bed below, to be covered, in time, with more sand and more coral. After the wood was gone there would be nothing left but the metal pieces caught here and there, and these would be so corroded they would not resemble a ship's skeleton. Without the clues in the cave, Rathe might never have located it.

She contented herself with watching him, the sunlight sending shafts of glittering gold light down from the surface, illuminating the air bubbles he sent up. She floated, weightless in their glow, watching too the multitudes of brightly colored fish that swam in and out of the coral formations, playing hide-and-seek with each other and with the dark divers who bubbled and invaded their way into previously undisturbed territory. The silence, the tranquility was ethereal, broken as Rathe tugged demandingly on her swim fin, directing her attention elsewhere. She followed him downward, through the coral labyrinth until they reached the bottom, a pastel prison of pink, mauve, deep violet, and rose stalagmites surrounding the sandy floor. There, a piece of equipment that she was unfamiliar with lay in the sand, and next to it, a slate to which a waxy-type writing implement was secured by a thin chain. It was this Rathe picked up, writing on it in bold, block letters.

"I VACUUM, YOU LOOK."

The piece of equipment, which turned out to be a large, industrial, complicated sort of vacuum, whooshed on, dragging at the sand voraciously wherever he pointed it, a screen that covered the front of its large hose stopping rocks and sandy pieces of coral and, very occasionally, something manmade.

The unfamiliar underwater work tired her far more easily than any above-water work would have done, and she glanced with growing frequency down to Rathe, who appeared to have a boundless supply of energy. She would have liked to interrupt his work for a break, but on second thought, the scowl was still evident, even under the mask, and so she did not. She hoped he would tire before she collapsed, though right now he was working at a furious pace, seemingly determined to make her scramble to keep up. She took courage from the fact that their air wouldn't last too much longer, forcing him to go up whether he wanted to or not.

Her pile of broken coral and rock grew, as did her little sack of encrusted stuff. What was it? It was very hard to tell until it had been cleaned. Most of the artifacts brought in to her had been at least partially cleaned beforehand. These were unknown quantities, their secrets hidden under a rough outer covering—like Rathe, she mused. If she was able to remove his ineffable, rough, defensive shell, what secrets would she find hidden within?

She stooped to retrieve a large object that the vacuum was furiously trying to gobble up with absolutely no success. She set the rather large cylindrical object aside and picked up the tablet.

"WHAT IS IT?" she wrote.

"CANNONBALL. UP," he answered. Terse, to the point, beyond the point of rudeness underwater, without words. That was some feat. Not that she expected flowery phrases on an eight-by-ten slate, but she suspected he was still angry anyway, accusing, condemning, and carrying out sentence for a crime he must know she couldn't commit. She broke the surface and removed her mask with a heartfelt sigh of relief. Her fingers trembled and she could barely manage to pull herself aboard, no thanks to Rathe! She gave him a dirty look. She could have been fish food for all he cared. He hadn't glanced back once to see how she fared, disappearing into the ship's cabin while she struggled to unbuckle her air tanks and remove the wet suit.

"This is ridiculous." Her fingers were numb and refused to undo the buckles and zippers.

"And entirely your own fault."

"Oh!" She dropped the buckles, allowing him to help her with them.

"Why didn't you tell me you were tired?" He handed her a steaming mug of liquid and a plate of sandwiches.

"Because I was already pretty sure you were aware of it, weren't you?" She knew he was a man of considerable acumen. "What is this?" She looked down at the cup, holding onto it tightly for the warmth.

He hung his feet off the side of the boat and took a sandwich from the plate, consuming a good third of it in one bite. "Coffee, cream, honey, and good Irish whiskey. Here . . ." He held the plate out to her. "Take a sandwich too; good for what ails you."

"The only thing ailing me is that you believe I ruined that vase." She had to discuss the matter with him, but it took courage. "You must believe me, no matter how upset I might have been, I wasn't really angry at you and, in any case, I would never take out my frustrations that way. That vase was the most beautiful thing I've ever seen."

"I know," he said simply.

"Rathe, it was intact after I left it at three in the morning, and if you don't believe that, at least you must admit that I wasn't breaking it around ten o'clock or even eleven last night."

He appeared to ponder this, breaking off pieces of his second sandwich and throwing the minute particles into the water, much to the delight of a growing number of small hungry fishes that congregated underneath.

"I know that, but Carmen could have been mistaken about the time."

Her spirits fell. Didn't he have enough regard for her

to take her word for it, or at the very least to give her the benefit of the doubt concerning the time? It would never occur to him that Carmen might have deliberately lied about the time to get Lorelei in trouble or that she might have been responsible for the damage itself.

"Besides, you're the only person I know who hates me enough to do that, aside from your father, and he isn't here or I would have suspected him first."

Now what did her father have to do with anything? "Rathe, I don't hate anyone that much and I certainly don't hate you." Far from it.

"No? Then I'd hate to see the shape you'd leave me in if you did."

"You're speaking about last night?"

"Only partly."

"I didn't mean to let anything happen..."

"And you succeeded very well in that goal. Nothing happened except that I was miserable all night."

For all that he was a grown man, he looked rather like a hungry little boy with his nose pressed against the candy-shop window, being told the store was closed for the day. She had to laugh at the accurate analogy and at the petulant set to his mouth.

"I don't see the humor."

She stifled the laugh. "So you think you were the only one last night to suffer? Where you get all your misinformation, I don't know."

He reached for her then, the anger evaporating like the water on his skin.

"It was no misconception that you wanted me as much as I wanted you last night. Why wouldn't you let me love you?"

"I didn't want you to." She couldn't meet his eyes with the untruth.

"Oh, yes you did. I thought you were passionate as a girl; that girl doesn't hold a candle to the woman I held in my arms last night. I never thought I'd want any woman the way I want you."

His voice and his proximity were intoxicating and she

set the cup down to move away from him. "Can't we forget that last night happened, at least for now, while we're both here on Andros?"

He followed her. "I don't understand you."

"That makes two of us." She focused her attention on the horizon, not wanting to meet his inquiring gaze. She had no answers for him or herself. Suddenly her attention was diverted. She wrinkled her brow curiously, the dilemma pushed into the background momentarily, as she scrutinized the dot, growing ever larger in the distance.

"Rathe, do you see anything out there?"

"Don't try to change the subject, Lorelei."

"No. I'm serious. I think I see a boat."

He pulled a pair of high-powered binoculars from a hook on the ship's wall. "You have very sharp eyes, my sweet." The binoculars were quickly stowed, as well as their diving gear, and Rathe unfolded two lawn chairs, placing them side by side on deck.

"Have a chair." He sounded relaxed, casual, but she could detect a note of wariness underneath. He was cautious about all boats, not that there were too many. Andros hadn't the regular tourist attractions or accomodations that some of the other islands did. Many of the mainstream tourists never made it this far, and if they did, they made for the island's guest resorts. This craft was making straight for them and wasn't the usual boat hired by divers intent only on a day's trek around the famous reef. This was an extremely expensive yacht, most definitely not of the rented variety.

The intruder drew nearer and as it did so, Rathe closed his eyes and slumped lower in the lounge chair as if he had nothing better to do than sun his muscular, tanned physique and sleep. He caressed the palm of her hand with his fingertips, tightening his hold when she would have pulled away.

"Relax and enjoy the view."

"Ahoy there! Good morning, folks!" The ship drew alongside theirs and a burly, overweight man with a shock of curling red hair swung himself aboard and walked toward them, his tennis shoes squeaking loudly as he approached.

"Morning." Rathe greeted the stranger in a neighborly tone. "What can I do for you?"

"Nothing much. Just being friendly...just being friendly."

"Well, we don't mind the company, Mr.—Mr.—"

"Wade. Joshua Wade, at your service."

Rathe clasped the proferred hand. "Rathe Drummond." He turned to her and helped her out of the chair. "Lorelei, why don't you go get Mr. Wade something cool to drink?"

She left for the refreshments, hiding her curiosity. Rathe saying he didn't mind the company? People in general were on Rathe's list of deadly sins, contact with whom had to be avoided at all costs. Why then the warm welcome?

She brought out the iced tea and another plate of sandwiches so thoughtfully left by Sarah yesterday in the refrigerator, placing them in front of Joshua Wade and another man, presumably from the same ship. Contrary to Mr. Wade's casual friendliness, this man, slight of build and very dark, seemed edgy and too quiet, reminding her of a scruffy fox terrier a long-ago neighbor had owned, a dog that snapped savagely at people when his owner wasn't looking.

In her absence Rathe had drawn up two more chairs and appeared to be engaging the men in an easygoing conversation—seemed to be, but wasn't. She could sense the agitation he felt and concealed just below a calm exterior. She had yet to see any problem that would completely unnerve Rathe, but these two men, for some reason, came closer to doing it than anyone else she knew of. She would have given a lot to know their technique. A horrible thought occurred to her then—the pirates! Rathe must suspect them to be somehow connected to the pirates. Were his suspicions justified?

"So you've been fishing, have you?"

She tuned herself back into the conversation.

"Fine fishing out here. Catch anything?"

"No." Rathe was obviously perturbed by the questions and the men whom he could not deal with in his usual abrupt and ofttimes rude manner.

She smiled to herself, a mischievous impulse pushing her toward a course of action she knew she would regret later. She couldn't give, *couldn't* give credence to what she knew he suspected, but something had to be done.

She spoke. "Actually, Mr. Wade, we did bring rods and reels, but we haven't used them. We've had much more important things to do, haven't we, dear?"

Rathe blanched visibly and the men leaned closer to her, hunched on the edges of their lawn chairs.

"Oh?" Mr. Wade's minion fidgeted excitedly.

"Yes, though it's all very...private, you understand." She could feel Rathe's gray eyes boring into her. It was time to put him out of his misery, or at least part of it. She smiled innocently at him.

"It's all right, sweetheart, these are grown men. They must know how it is with newlyweds, how nothing is quite so important...quite so private...as getting to know each other." She smiled suggestively at all three and bent her head to kiss Rathe on the cheek, allowing a curtain of dark hair to hide the probable shock on his face. It was his turn to be in an uncomfortable position with no power whatsoever to change it.

Joshua Wade leaned back in his chair, his expression openly leering as he took in Lorelei's shapely figure, shown to advantage in the fire-red suit. "Why, Mr. Drummond, if I had me a wife as pretty as yours, I'd sure take her somewhere better than this place to show her off."

"Precisely why I chose Andros, gentlemen. Having a...wife who looks like this, imagine how little time I would have her to myself if I took her to say, Nassau. This way we can, as she put it, get to know each other with only occasional invasions of privacy."

The other man tensed. "You mean those little boats we saw shuttling back and forth from the island?"

Rathe shrugged philosophically. "My in-laws. Can't live with them or without them it seems. My uncle owns a house a ways inland, owns this boat too. He gave it to us for our honeymoon so we could get away from it all. So far, we haven't been able to get away from him or my cousins. Every day they're here offering to show us the sights or invite us to dinner. You'd think my uncle never had a honeymoon." Rathe laughed.

"I'm sure he doesn't want you to get bored and, you know, there are quite a few interesting things to do here. There's always diving. Did you know you're floating on top of one of the world's most famous coral reefs?" Mr. Wade was a fountain of helpful information.

"No kidding?"

Rathe looked genuinely interested—a consummate actor, and she could have sworn he was serious, as serious as he sounded about their supposed marriage. She was beginning to regret that bit of foolishness. Even if it worked, there would be hell to pay later.

"You mean you haven't done any diving?"

Could they have seen the dripping wet diving gear? Lorelei thought not, but she too was starting to become uneasy at the line of questioning. Perhaps they had already been down and were trying to verify if anyone else had. She put on her best imitation of a seductive voice.

"Why, Mr. Wade, we do have the gear. My husband's cousins loaned us some, but I'm sure you can understand why we haven't found the time to do too much of anything out-of-doors. Besides—" She pouted. "I'm not sure if I want my husband to do any diving. Do you think there might be something down there more interesting to him than I am? We only have a short honeymoon and I surely wouldn't want to be left all alone on it."

The redhead wet his lips. "No, ma'am. Nothing down there would be as interesting as you are."

"Are you sure?" she insisted. "I mean, have you checked recently?"

"Not lately." Red admitted.

"Good." Rathe mumbled it to himself but the smaller man heard.

"What?"

Lorelei stood, smoothing imaginary lines from her bathing-suit bottom, drawing the attention from Rathe. "What my husband means—" she threw him a knowing look, "—what he means is that I have this tendency to swim in the nude, and he's so terribly old-fashioned about spectators."

Both visitors swallowed simultaneously, Rathe's provoking comment gone from their minds. She stretched her arms over her head and yawned pointedly. It was high time for them to leave.

"If you gentlemen would excuse me; it has been very nice to meet you, but my morning has been so long that I think I'll take a nice nap; my bed seems so inviting." She winked broadly at Rathe as she left them, her hips undulating suggestively. They'd get that hint and leave, or give Rathe ample reason to ask them to go.

She closed the galley door and indecisively eyed the radio Rathe had left there. The impromptu plan had worked, but only so long as none of their "cousins" showed up for work. She picked up the mike and clicked the radio on, but a hand closed over hers before she could speak into the device, tearing the transmitter from her grasp.

"Honeymoon's over, huh?" she asked, but his face was a dark mask. Where was his sense of humor?

"Lorelei, I was trying to get rid of them, not convince them to stay. What in hell were you doing out there?"

"Trying to help you get rid of them and allay suspicion?"

He shook his head in disbelief. "I was doing that when you started with the come-hither looks and threatening to swim nude. Good Lord, woman, I'll never get rid of them now."

If she didn't know better she would have said he was

jealous, but she knew that he was only angry that she had taken things out of his hands. She pointed to the window smugly. "They're gone, aren't they?"

"They'll be back."

Thankfully, her actions fell lower on his list of worries than the two men in their expensive yacht. "The pirates, you think?" She poured him a cup of the coffee-whiskey combination from the thermos.

He refused it curtly. "No thanks. I need all my wits about me when I'm around you. And, yes, I think they might be. They fit the latest description. The trouble is, whoever is in charge is smart. They hire a couple of men to do the jobs a few times, then get new ones, so I can't be absolutely sure."

"Rathe, don't you think it's possible you might have blown this thing all out of proportion, looking for problems that aren't there? I admit they weren't exactly pleasant, but I've met a lot of people who were unpleasant and nosy, but that's a long way from piracy."

"Interested in defending them, aren't you? And by the way, what were you doing with the radio? Never mind . . ." he ordered. "Bring the bag of artifacts. We're going in."

"Don't you think we'd better wait until they're out of sight? We did say we might be doing . . . other things."

"You said it, I didn't, and if you think I'll let you make a fool of me in private as well as in public, you're sadly mistaken. I won't give you the opportunity to repeat that little performance again. I hate it when you parade around pretending to be something you're not." At her look of confusion he continued in explanation: "Not that this dramatization was any more ridiculous than the one I saw you put on the night of your fancy engagement party. They were both equally phony." He shouldered the bag of artifacts. "You know, Lorelei, I had high hopes that living and working among real, down-to-earth people here on Andros might put you back in touch with yourself; I was beginning to think it had."

"Back there was a ruse. Don't you see, I was trying to help you."

He shook a warning finger at her. "If I ever do marry, I won't be using my wife's body to avoid trouble or to buy . . . whatever it was you were trying to buy out there."

"I was trying to buy you time, to get their minds off some of your stupid comments about their diving." His ungratefulness astounded her.

"Don't do me any favors, woman! Your imitation of what my wife would be like, of how she would behave, humiliated me. Am I supposed to be grateful for that? Stavros may want a wife like that; I do not. She is calculating, manipulative, brittle, sophisticated maybe, seductive maybe, but she doesn't seduce me . . . she disgusts me."

Her lower lip trembled with hurt and rage. "I apologize for pretending to be your wife. I should have known you would have impossibly high standards that I could never hope to achieve."

"The only standard, the only requirement I want from my wife would be love, and you're right, you couldn't give that to me. You're saving yourself for a man who feels no passion for you, who wants you because he needs a lovely figurehead, a hostess, maybe a mother for the Halkias heirs. But he doesn't love you. It isn't his fault; he's never been in love and he doesn't know there's anything more to feel. He hasn't been brought up to expect more. But you know, and you're planning to go through with the marriage anyway. He might be happy with the kind of affection you can give him; but he won't make you happy. He can't."

How like him to ruin her hopes with a few well-chosen words. "And what do you have, a crystal ball to see into my future? Can you propose another path that would make me happier?" He was giving her nothing but orders, he had no better alternative for her except a life alone; and even a passionless marriage, a lukewarm love must be better than spending the rest of one's life in solitude.

"I suggested another path for you six years ago, but you refused it. The offer still stands, but if you want to do things that way, you'll have to come to me. I won't do the asking again."

One man's figurehead, another's mistress. Some choice.

She sat silently brooding and thoughtful as they sped to shore, close to him in body but not in spirit. It set a precedent for the weeks ahead.

CHAPTER TEN

RATHE DOUBLED THEIR work schedules in fear that the two men would decide to come back and set up camp before the majority of the artifacts could be salvaged. He partnered two divers to a team that worked together, side by side, for the better part of sixteen hours a day, and slept together, figuratively, for the rest of the night, it taking too much time to shuttle back and forth between the boat and the island for food, sleep, and changes of clothes. The close quarters and awkward sleeping arrangements contributed to the tension already present in abundance, and it didn't help matters any that Rathe had taken Lorelei off cataloguing duties for the time being, insisting she work beside him as his partner, adding fuel to Carmen's hatred and making everyone else distinctly uncomfortable. Not that Carmen need have worried. Rathe's mind, as far as she could tell, was devoid of any thoughts of intimacy, his total concentration on getting the artifacts up and into the house before his premonition of disaster was realized.

The hour was late, the divers weary and tense, tired of bitter coffee, cold food and colder showers, and most of all each other and the boat that had become their purgatory.

Not wanting a mutiny on his hands, or maybe wanting some of Lucy's cooking himself, Rathe led the hungry pack to the plantation and to a dinner of thick clam chowder, red snapper filets in anchovy sauce, and mounds of pineapple, mango, and banana fruit salad. Full, they lounged around the dinner table in silence until a frenzied knocking at the outer door sounded and Lucy admitted a sea of eager faces, complete with flash cameras, tape recorders, and unanswered questions.

"Mr. Drummond, is it true you've discovered the remains of a seventeenth-century Spanish galleon near Andros?" The question was directed to Rathe.

"And that there's at least a quarter million dollars aboard her in silver bar?" This from an American reporter with a Midwest twang.

The cameras flashed again. "And that you've tried to keep this thing under wraps because you don't have government authorization to do the salvaging?"

"Exactly where is this galleon? Can you take us there tonight?" They swarmed like grunion, stepping on and over one another in their attempt to reach Rathe.

He answered them so quietly that the room was instantly hushed to catch his words. "Before I answer any of your questions, gentlemen, I must know where you got this information, and if I do *not* get the answer to that question, I guarantee you won't get the answers to yours."

A slight, youthful young man with a mop of curly blond hair elbowed his way to the front. "That's easy. A friend of a friend of mine on Nassau relayed a message he received a week ago." He checked the scribble wrtten on a battered note pad. "It was from a woman, name of . . . Lorelei Averill."

The hours that followed were a nightmare of chaos, with Rathe barking orders to the crew and reporters alike, the latter still scurrying back and forth in an attempt to pry information from any available source, since Rathe's answers to their questions had been anything but informative. With a sharp-tongued Carmen barricading the artifact room and a tight-lipped Taylor manning the front door, though, their efforts were as unproductive as anyone could hope for under the circumstances and the disappointed menagerie was finally evicted from the premises late that afternoon. It wasn't much of a victory, for though he could keep them from setting foot on the property, he couldn't keep them from bobbing up and down like determined corks in their flotilla of rented boats just offshore. In the end, just after sunset, Mother Nature managed to convince the reporters that a night spent on the water, without food, light, heat, water, or comfort facilities was less than desirable, dampening their dogged persistence at least until the morning. It was a respite, and one that the crew were all grateful for, but it was only a temporary reprieve. They all knew that by tomorrow the enemy camp would be better organized, the first half-informed, overeager wave of recruits replaced by professional divers, photographers, newspaper people, and speculators—anyone, in fact, with an interest in the treasure who could beg, borrow, or rent a boat and a pair of swim fins.

There was no time to waste in cross-examining Lorelei, though she had the support of the majority of the crew; no time to bring the artifacts up with regard and deliberation, to clean and examine, to classify or photograph, to savor the flavor of their mutual success. They worked in human assembly lines, speed replacing all other values, with everyone, even inexperienced Sarah who, thanks to Stavros, had a few weeks of pleasure diving to her credit, pressed into service. The only one remaining on land was Lucy, left to guard the home front and the disordered artifact room that soon bulged to overflowing with a jungle of coral-encrusted objects that were warehoused in stacks and mounds, overlapping onto each other and up the walls; ancient, rusting saber blades and ballast bricks crushed alongside fragile bone haircombs.

The disruption of their normal schedule was a pity, and if the reporter's statements were to be believed, Lorelei's fault. And it hadn't helped for Rathe to remember that he had caught her, with the radio in her hand, aboard ship.

Lorelei hastily rebraided her hair and tossed the salt-water soaked plait back out of the way, careful to keep her balance in the heavily burdened boat. Against his own explicit decree, Rathe was under the water alone, frantically collecting whatever he could to bring up and toss in her already well-laden boat. Safety, it appeared, was for yesterday, before the reporters came. She tried to still the worry that gnawed, irrationally, at the back of her mind. He wasn't really down there alone. Taylor and Stavros were there too, somewhere, though probably they were not within sight of one another, each responsible for making sure a particular quadrant was picked as clean as possible of any artifacts, each man's position marked by the boat that acted as a buoy and collection depot above him. Still, Rathe had been down for an awfully long time. She eyed her watch anxiously, glancing distastefully at Carmen, some distance away, who kept vigil over Taylor, and at Sarah, who did the same for Stavros. Each had her hands full with her own responsibilities and would not be able to help her, but she would signal them, in any case, if she had to go down and look for him.

A bubbling and a spray of water startled her into awareness, rendering her problem hypothetical.

"Are you okay?" She pressed the tired diver for an answer. "You were down much too long. I was beginning to get worried."

"How touching," he responded in weary sarcasm, throwing his gear aboard. "Our modern-day Judas feels remorse."

She helped him aboard, a thing he allowed her to do out of necessity but with evident distaste. His body quivered with the effort he demanded of it.

She stood, hands on hips in exasperation. "The human body isn't made to take the kind of grueling punishment you dish out, Rathe, and while I grant that you may not be human, the rest of us are. Have a heart."

He flicked the radio on. "Carmen? Sarah? Rathe here. We're full and we're going on in. When Taylor and Stavros come up, follow us to the house. We'll take a break and discuss progress from there."

Progress was better than anyone had expected, as Ed, who had been transporting the artifacts—shuttling to and from the site all night long, trading an emptied boat for a full one—told them. He'd given up on the artifact room and had turned the living room into a larger version of the room upstairs. They sat cross-legged on the carpeting now covered with salvage and sandy brown muck, each with a plate of sandwiches and an urn of something warm to drink.

Rathe crossed out large sections on the map before him, indicating in black ink those sections finished, in red those remaining. "We've done well . . . just how well I'll be able to tell you in a minute." He scrawled more information in a note pad beside him while the rest of the group sat quietly, conversing in voices lethargic with fatigue, keeping their eyes open and their coffee cups filled being all the activity they could handle at one time.

Rathe tossed the papers down. "The way it looks, we won't get to sleep for a week." He hardened himself to the chorus of moans. "I want the same teams to pair up, but this time, the ones topside go under, except for Sarah." He paused remorsefully upon seeing her drooping shoulders. Working with the others had matured her a great deal. The painfully shy girl had turned into a woman, and a crew member who wanted to prove she could pull her own weight with the best of them.

Rathe handled that fragile ego gently. "Sarah, I'm only replacing you with Ed because he hasn't had as much down time as we have. The problem is, that leaves us with no one to transport."

"I can sail, Rathe," she stated confidently. "You know I can."

The strategy worked. "I don't want to draft you . . ."

"You wouldn't have to draft anyone if it weren't for *her*." Carmen hadn't contributed much to the conversation, preferring to sit silently brooding at Rathe's side, smoking cigarette after cigarette and sending hateful looks at Lorelei. "I don't know why you don't send her away. She can't do any more damage to us now if she goes, and she might do more if she stays."

"I need every hand I can get; besides, she's working with me."

"She's working against you! Do you need more proof?"

"Enough!" Lucy humphed at them all like a banty hen with ruffled feathers.

"I don't think it is." Ed voiced his opinion for the first time. "Your irrational dislikes don't count as facts here yet, Carmen."

"You want the facts?" she shrilled. "The facts are—"

"That you're a jealous, vindictive—"

"*Enough!*" Taylor roared. "Mrs. Yates said enough!" He fixed an icy stare on Carmen, then his son. "And I'll have no more of that kind of talk. We pull together in this or it falls apart about our ears. We've no time for bickering. We can get this thing done before the reporters come if we try."

"Want to make any bets?" Carmen pointed to Stavros who had closed his eyes and assumed a prone position, his blond, tossled head resting on Sarah's shoulder. Both were sound asleep.

Rathe groaned and rubbed his eyes wishfully. "I guess that's it then." He stopped Taylor who would have awakened his daughter. "No, no, no, don't wake them. We aren't machines. I've expected too much."

Taylor sounded gruff and sleepy. "I'm sorry things are turning out this way, boy, but I'm glad to hear you finally admitting it."

Lorelei watched with mixed feelings as they climbed the stairs. With Stavros and Sarah asleep, and Taylor and Lucy fast joining them, Rathe's hopes of salvaging the remainder of his galleon vanished. It was early morning now; soon the island would be swarming with people, all eager to steal a piece of Rathe's private pie. He might forgive her for his lost sleep, for the horrifying amount of work they'd had to do in such a short time, but he would not forgive her if it had all been for nothing, if he had to stand by impotently and watch as everything he had worked so hard during the past six years to achieve was poached right before his eyes. His hopes faded with each passing minute and so did hers.

She left him crouched down on the floor, discouraged, the sheaf of unsalvaged quadrants still in his hand; she had work to do. The morning was clear and the seabirds were out in all their squawking splendor, and she wasn't aware that she was being followed until she felt a hand on her shoulder. She turned around to confront Rathe.

"Where do you think you're going?"

"Back out."

She saw a minute flicker of hope ignite and then die. "Why . . . to guide your friends in?"

"Think what you will." He was beyond reason, and she hadn't the strength to change his mind. She could only pray she had the strength left to do what had to be done. "I'm going back out."

He moved around to stand in front of her, halting her progress. "This is crazy. I don't know what you think you're doing, but you don't even have the list of the quadrants that need going over."

"But you do." She gazed up at him honestly, willing him to come with her.

"It would be very, very hard work." He hesitated.

"Less if there were two or more." She wasn't giving up on his dream even if she had to do it alone.

"Carmen can watch the house while the others sleep, but if we take Ed with us in our boat, there won't be room for as many artifacts; if we take two boats, or we go back and forth from the site to the island, there's a greater chance of being spotted. If we go, it will be just the two of us, out there alone, until the job is finished."

"I'm going," she repeated firmly. "Are you coming with me?"

The hours passed, nine, ten, eleven o'clock, as Lorelei and Rathe each took an area to work in, the boat anchored above them, stopping only long enough for stimulating, reviving sips of coffee and to change air tanks. Fortunately the grid they searched was close to the surface here, making the work relatively easy.

She brushed away a grouper that seemed determined to hide in the silky tresses of her hair and took one last look around the area. The space looked clean, though it might not be, hiding secrets still, embedded in the coral. It could be checked over at another time for any straggling pieces. For now, she was going up. She signaled Rathe and ascended the few feet to the surface, leaning against the boat, clinging to its side for support until she could muster the energy to climb aboard. She felt weak and nauseated from the exertion and, moving the already collected artifacts aside, took advantage of the empty space.

The little motorboat's metal bottom was wet and gritty and smelled of fish, its surface cold and uninviting against her skin, but it was a measure of how tired she was that she lay down upon it anyway, using her air tanks as a pillow, hanging her legs over the side, not even bothering to remove her fins. When Rathe came up, as he had signaled he would within five minutes, she would have to have a talk with him. No amount of wrongly assumed guilt could force her to go on with this madness. She needed sleep, they both did, and somehow she had to convince Rathe to believe it. She wasn't suggesting they give up, but a few hours' rest . . .

The radio bleeped into life and she answered its call sleepily, her tongue thick in her mouth, her every movement sluggish. She must have dozed off.

"Lorelei here," she said into the mike. "Ed? Is that you? Would you repeat that last transmission please? I

didn't get it." The radio snapped and crackled in mean-
ingless static as she waited.

"It's Ed," the voice repeated. "Lorelei, I need to speak
to Rathe right away. There's trouble."

She pushed the button to send. "Sorry, Ed. No can
do. He's still down. Give me the message and I'll see
that... hang on a second."

Bubbles boiled to the surface indicating his approach
and she handed the radio to Rathe, taking the mask from
his face herself, dropping it into the boat.

"It's Ed. It sounds urgent."

He wiped the water from his face and keyed the button. "Fill me in, Ed. What's the trouble?" He sounded
alert, prepared for whatever Ed had to tell him, and
despite herself, she couldn't help but admire the man.

She drew her gaze from his muscular shoulders, glis-
tening with bright drops of water, and concentrated her
somewhat limited attention to what the two men were
saying.

"The reporters are back and they've brought rein-
forcements, ah, but they don't know where the site is
and they don't know where you are."

"For God's sake, don't tell them."

There was a pause at the other end of the line. "I
couldn't Rathe; I don't know where you are, but...
well... there are those here who would like to know.
You know... Carmen..."

"I've gone to the blue hole," Rathe, grown even more
wary, deliberately misled the younger man, "but, Ed,
don't tell her that and don't contact me out here again
if you can avoid it. We sit low in the water, and they
haven't seen us yet. I don't want to be tracked through
communications."

There was no reply; Ed followed orders well.

"They're going to get tired of waiting and they're
going to come looking for us, won't they?" she asked
in dismay.

"Yes! And when they find us, it's all over." His frustration and worry could be seen in the pucker between his brows and the way his fists were clenched tightly together unconsciously.

"We could hire guards then to patrol the site area while we work," she suggested. "I know it isn't the ideal solution, but we would be free to work and bring up the rest of the cargo in safety."

"It isn't just that." He was silent for a moment. "Do you know that over one hundred men lost their lives and went down with this galleon? A hundred individuals with parents and wives and children who waited for news that must have taken months or even years to reach them. There were no services said or prayers offered for the sailors because the bodies were gone, buried at sea. There were no flowers or markers, only the galleon; their tomb, their only monument. The man who owned the *Princess* never gave up hope that his son would be found alive. Three hundred years later I found proof that he died, with his ship; a gold medallion, very small, very fragile, and it could have been ruined beyond recognition by one clumsy foot. When I disinter what remains of their lives, I want to do it privately, or with people who care as much as I do, not with a pack of grave robbers, who could care less about anything but a sensational story or a souvenir, tromping over what's left of them." His eyes were trained to the shore as he talked, on the tiny boats that, from this distance, resembled so many army ants milling around in a stirred-up nest.

"But what can we do to prevent it?" she asked him helplessly. "We can't salvage all that there's left to salvage today, just the two of us. We'll be lucky if we're able to get the chest out of the blue hole without their spotting us."

"I've thought of that, and I have an idea." He studied her thoughtfully. "We'll wait until dark so they can't track us by sight before we start the engine. We'll head for the blue hole; you'll drop me off there and then you'll head for shore, just below the plantation, away from the dock, and head for the house with the rest of the artifacts that way."

"Alone? You want me to leave you to salvage the blue-hole chest alone?" She clearly remembered the lecture Taylor had received for just that offense. "Even you can't possibly value this project above your life. What do you want to do, end up in the same place as our Spanish sailors?"

"I'm afraid it's the only way, Lorelei." He prepared for an argument.

"You aren't thinking clearly. I could come with you; we could do this together. It would be easier and safer and we could leave the boat here. Go now, if you're worried the motor would attract their attention, and swim back with the chest later."

"And leave this boat right here to lead them to our main site?"

She hadn't thought about that. "Whatever we're going to do, we'd better do it now. Rathe, here they come."

The boats began to swarm away from the crowded dock, making a beeline in their direction.

"It isn't safe for you to come with me." He jumped into the water, buckling his gear on the run. "Now go; lead them a merry chase away from here if you can."

"I can't leave you."

"*Go!* I'm your employer, Lorelei, and I'm ordering you to get out of here and back to shore."

"If you don't trust me to—"

He broke in. "It isn't that. It's a long swim to the hole from here, and there's a great deal to be accomplished before I can head for shore myself. The truth is, I won't have enough air in my tanks to do it under oxygen. That will mean swimming through the reefs, after dark without tanks, carrying whatever artifacts I find that are too valuable to be left behind. It isn't safe for me, let alone you."

"You were the one yelling at me for trying to change my leopard's spots, for allowing myself to be swathed in cotton wool and protected from life's little excitements. You're the hypocrite. I could help you, and if you're willing to take the risks, so am I."

"No." He was every bit as bullheaded as she. "You won't change my mind and if I stay to convince you, they'll be upon us and we'll both lose. Please, if you care at all, lead them away from me, and get back to shore."

"Bury these, I won't be able to take them." She tossed him the burlap bag of artifacts and sped away from him, heading out to sea. Little did her pursuers know that they followed an empty boat, Lorelei already over the side, doubling back after the man she refused to let go.

CHAPTER ELEVEN

THE USUALLY CLEAR, transparent sea had darkened and would grow murkier as night approached, but even so, as she neared the blue hole, the water seemed even more forbidding. Fingers of black coral reached out for her, color-muted sponges took on alien, ominous personalities, and despite her put-on bravado for Rathe, she would give a lot to be able to find him.

As suddenly as she wished it, he appeared below her, streaking toward her and dragging to the surface a small pouch of artifacts held under his arm.

"What in the world are you doing here? I thought I told you to lead them away and then get yourself back to shore?"

She could just make out the expression on his face in the dusky light. He was worried, not angry. "I did lead them away, out to sea to be exact, but I jumped out some time before they caught up to me and I am going back to shore, with you."

"Stubborn . . . willful . . . obstinate woman." He sputtered with the water, his mouthpiece half on and half off.

"I thought you wanted me to be that way—spirited, I think you said."

"Foolhardy, and it's not the same. Lorelei, I could strangle you."

"No, you couldn't, your hands are full. And besides, I swim faster."

He tread water angrily, refusing to be placated. "You won't go back to shore without me?"

"No."

"Then we'll both have to go back now, while we still have air, and abandon the blue-hole chest. I can't risk taking you there under these conditions. Do you have any idea what your father and Stavros would do to me if I allowed you to come to harm? Don't you see what choices you're forcing me to make?"

She did; she was asking him to chose either her or his project and she wasn't sure if she would like the answer, no matter which of them he chose. It wasn't a decision she wanted him to have to make, so without further discussion, she put the mask over her face and, clamping the mouthpiece tightly between her teeth, dove straight down into the hole, scattering a school of fish in her haste.

The chest that could be seen through the small boat's skeleton had largely decomposed, its shape retained by the living fossils of coral, a petrified replica of the original container. Rathe reached her side and brushed her out of the way, chipping in frenzied haste at the bonds that held the box to the shelf, marring its surface. He tilted it slightly on its side to judge its weight; with his concentration on the box, he failed to see the rectangular-shaped object, glittering with gold and light, that slipped through an opening in the bottom and headed down into the abyss.

Lorelei did see it and, unmindful of the consequences, hurtled down after it into the dark strangeness of cold water and jagged-edged coral. She managed to hold it until Rathe came to help her, and together they maneuvered the little box to the surface. Preserved by its outer chest from the ravages of the tides and curious fish, the small rectangular box was beautiful. Exquisitely constructed of ivory, its sides were inlaid with mother-of-pearl and decorated with intricate flower designs made up of gold and jade and pearl clusters. And inside . . . Rathe lifted the lid and tilted the box to allow the accummulated water to escape. He did not touch the box's contents, but closed the lid again, his eyes wide in awe.

Lorelei swallowed, the moisture gone from her mouth. Here was the treasure lost to the galleon, the treasure the men had died trying to save—pearls, jade, gold, ivory, emeralds, diamonds, and more precious and semiprecious stones of all kinds than Lorelei had ever seen, set in rings, necklaces, bracelets, and all manner of feminine adornment.

"Here it is," he whispered to her. "Now all we have to do is get it to shore."

Getting to shore proved to be as difficult as Rathe suspected, their air predictably running out well before they could stand up in the water. They had to discard the bulky, heavy oxygen tanks and swim for it, carrying the box and the pouch of artifacts together. It was an awkward swimming position that enervated them and left them gasping for ragged breaths of air once they reached the shore just below the plantation.

"Gifts for a Spanish princess," he whispered when he could speak again. "For the future Queen of Spain, from a man who never had the chance to present his gifts and pay his homage to her."

"You knew this was down there?"

"I knew it was supposed to be, though even I had no idea the wealth would be this considerable. The boy's father made mention of jewels; lord, he must have saved for a lifetime, two lifetimes to amass this much. But since the journey itself was begun in secret, there was no direct mention of the jewels in the manifest. The young man's suit wasn't favored by everyone, so I imagine he wanted this to be a surprise."

"So she never knew that he loved her?" There was a sadness about that; it touched her.

He shrugged, uncertain. "Maybe she did. Maybe it was she who sent him to his death trying to bring her the sun, moon, and stars, hoping that if he laid the world at her feet, it would be enough to buy her love; perhaps he was not the man her royal father wanted her to wed, and so she could not acknowledge his suit."

"You don't look on the bright side, do you? Rathe, I..."

"Hush." He shook his head and put a finger to her mouth. "I haven't thanked you for saving it for me. It could never have been replaced."

"Maybe now you'll believe I didn't have a hand in trying to take it from you."

He opened the case and withdrew an amethyst pendant on a long, pure gold chain. The stone gleamed richly in the moonlight as he held it out to her.

"Take it, please I want you to have it."

She shook her head no, her hair falling down about her bare shoulders. A part of her being wanted to accept the gift, but there was another part that held back. It wasn't the kind of gift she wanted. The pendant was merely payment for services rendered above and beyond the call of duty. It contained nothing of him but gratitude, and she didn't want that.

"I can't accept it."

He placed it on her neck anyway, in defiance of her wishes. "You can tell your fiancé you found it, if you don't want him to know that I gave it to you. Am I to be allowed nothing? Consider it a gift from our Spanish sailor." He touched her hair, seal-slick from the water. "No Spanish princess could have had hair so ebony black or eyes so emerald green, or skin so soft that a man is drawn to touch it even though he's sworn to himself that he must not. No princess could have been more worthy to wear this treasure." He lifted the pendant from where it rested in the hollow of her throat, fingering its simple elegance.

She could barely hear him but she could feel the heat of his fingers as they hovered so near her skin in the semidarkness. This was madness, it was wrong; but if it were, her value system needed updating badly. She reached for him, pulling his wet body to her, unresisting.

"Hold me. Don't talk, just hold me, please."

His hands journeyed sensuously from her shoulders, down one side of her waist to caress the tender flesh of her inner thigh, then stopped, unmoving. "I'd like nothing beter than to lie here, on the sand, and love you, and love you, and love you until I became the center of your entire existence, but I can't do it with an audience." He pushed her gently away as a high-powered boat chugged its way to where they stood and turned on the spotlight.

"There they are!"

"Pull into shore here. We can drag the boats up onto the beach."

"Drummond, is that you?"

"Hey! What're you carrying under your arm?"

Rathe held the box tighter to his body and directed his comments to her, ignoring the reporter's questions altogether. "It's a good thing I don't believe in an unchangeable fate. Do you know, every tme I've tried to hold you, something has happened to prevent it? It could make a man superstitious."

"But not you?" She touched the amethyst pendant. "Haven't you ever accepted something the way it was, just because there was nothing at all you could do to change it?"

"Once," he admitted. "And I've regretted it ever since. I should have tried harder . . . to change things. But since, I've become the master of my own destiny. It's a philosophy, a way of looking at things that I highly recommend."

She looked from the trees behind them to the water in front. "I've found that sometimes the decision is taken out of your hands. Like now, master of our destiny. How do you propose dealing with them to your advantage? I suppose we could just wait for them to catch up to us and then refuse to discuss the ship or her contents."

The reporters she referred to were already making a wobbly attempt to land.

He lifted her to her feet and took her hand. "I don't think that would work. Even if they are only reporters, speculators, and prospective buyers, from the looks of them, they would kill to get their hands on a genuine artifact and the story to go along with it." He added cryptically, "And I'm only half in jest about that last part. Come on, let's go."

The entire soggy gaggle was left behind, their landing without benefit of lights or experience, a comedy of errors Lorelei would have given a great deal to see if she had not been a part of their intended prey. Their noisy squawking grew dim in the distance.

"Did you see them? They capsized two boats in trying to beach the one, and it didn't look as if that was the first time. Oh, for a movie camera . . . we'd make a fortune. Speaking of cameras, what do you think the dunking will do to the film?"

"The same thing it's going to do their two-hundred-dollar suits and their blow-dried haircuts."

She broke into laughter. "That should teach them."

"What are you laughing about, funny face? You don't look any better. They'd throw you out of your fancy marina club looking like that."

She picked a piece of vine that trailed from his swim trunks. "At least I'd have company. They wouldn't let you in either."

"I don't want in . . . in the marina anyway. I *do* want in the plantation house though, so if you're through discussing the merits of our wardrobes, will you please move your pretty long legs faster?"

"I'm running as fast as I can," she grumbled. "It would help if you tried to locate a trail . . . not blaze one."

"All the established routes will be covered."

"All right." She winced as a thin tree branch whipped across her face. "But I'm not a bulldozer, you know."

She stumbled over his feet, causing the sack under her arm to slip, spilling its contents over the ground.

"Whose side are you on, woman?" He helped her toss artifacts, rocks, and pieces of vegetation back into the sack.

"My own. It seems I have to look out for myself. No one else is."

"If you feel that way, I can leave you to your own devices." He threw the threat back to her in exasperation.

"No, no, no, no. I don't want you to leave me alone."

"Then stop complaining and utilize some of the energy in running that you're wasting telling me you can't run!"

He slapped her on the bottom and pushed her over the top of a massive boulder, dragging himself up behind, pulling himself up by her ankle.

"Surely they aren't still following us?" She crouched on the rock and peered over the edge.

"I don't know." He looked doubtful. "Nothing much seems to stop them . . . neither rain nor gloom of night, or however that goes."

"Where are your trained boars when you need them?"

"It sounds like they could be right . . . over . . . there." He pointed to a rustling in the brush. "But I bet you dollars to donuts that isn't boar. It's either their advance scouts or their rear guard." He frowned. "So far they don't know about the chest. I would rather they didn't and I might be able to get past them . . . but it will be harder to do with two."

"So? Go alone. Even if they do catch up with me, what can they find?" She extracted a handful of items from the pouch. "If they're willing to risk trouble with you to get their hands on a round thingamajig or an oblong whatnot, let them." The items were uncleaned and to the untrained eye could easily pass for dirt clods, especially after they had been dropped in the soil. "I don't need you," she said convincingly.

He kissed her quickly. "We'll discuss that in greater detail later. I'll see you at the house. Take care."

She pushed him to greater speed and stumbled her way ahead alone, leaving two trails for their persistent invaders to follow, hers leading to the kitchen door, the only door not barricaded by a garrison of onlookers. Inside, throngs of people milled about—crew members, reporters, pirates, vandals, for all she knew or cared. She found her way unmolested into Rathe's private study and slumped down into an overstuffed leather recliner, using her pouch of artifacts for a lumpy pillow, to await Rathe or the reporters, whoever came first.

As it happened, neither came, the reporters having been ushered out along with all nonauthorized personnel some hours before dawn. It was her own stomach grumbling and the smell of breakfast cooking that roused Lorelei some hours later.

She paraded into the kitchen, a bedraggled thing with her long hair in knots and her bathing suit covered with humus and sand. Stavros, who was manning a frying pan full of bacon, left his post to kiss her temple.

"Morning, sweetheart. We heard you had a rough night of it." He kissed her again, and to her horror, she shied away from him.

"And from the looks of me, it was worse than anybody let on, right?" she grumbled testily.

"I'm sorry we all abandoned you yesterday. We heard you and Rathe did it all." He spoke apologetically, believing he knew the reason for her grumpiness.

"Did . . . did Rathe tell you that?" She faltered at his name. Where was he this morning? She fought the urge to ask that of Stavros.

"No. Carmen said something about it just a few minutes ago."

So he was with Carmen, or had at least talked with her sometime between last night and this morning. She drank the small glass of freshly squeezed orange juice Sarah placed before her.

She poured herself another cup of coffee, leaving it undiluted by sugar or cream. "I'm going upstairs for a shower and a change of clothes. Don't bother waiting breakfast for me."

She could hear Rathe moving about in his bedroom. Had he gotten any sleep? Where had he put the box that no one seemed to know anything about yet? Quickly she opened his door. It came to her later that in her exuberance to see him, she should have knocked before entering the domain of his bedroom. Not that it would have altered things dramatically, though it might have given Carmen time to get up from his bed; that is, if she had cared two cents about appearances, which Lorelei didn't think she did.

She didn't know how long she stood there, staring, before Taylor pulled her away; not long, but long enough to imprint the picture in her mind. Rathe was asleep, deeply asleep, with his arms flung wide, his hair matted and falling down over his face. Carmen was not asleep, looking like a cat with a bowl of cream as she lay, covered to her chin, in Rathe's blankets.

"It's not what you're thinking girl." Taylor read her mind and answered it. "I've eyes in my head and I see nothing between them."

"Not even a wall."

"Ah, don't let it make you bitter, and don't let it blind you to the truth. She was downstairs, eating a big breakfast, not half an hour ago, and you don't fall asleep and wake up looking like that in a few minutes' time."

"She was in his bed, Taylor!" She couldn't keep the pain from her voice and somehow didn't mind that Taylor knew. "Taylor, what am I going to do now?" She sobbed and let him hold her against the rough material of his shirt.

"Talk to him, lass, talk to him. There's something fishy in there and you mark my words. Don't let it spoil what you have between you."

"I have no right to care one way or another, you know that."

"That I do." He was a perceptive man. "Stavros is a good boy and he'll make some woman a fine husband someday, a very fine husband. But men are a little like ships, don't you see, and Stavros is like a ship that's made to sail in smooth, shallow lake water. He cannot handle the open sea. It takes a special ship to do that, with the right man at her helm." He walked with her down the stairs, slowly, his voice as weathered as himself and as full of color. "A woman can get in a man's blood, just like the sea can, if she's a special woman. Once a man has tasted her, he cannot free himself. He loves her at times, he hates her at times, but he's true to her, yes he is, and he cannot leave her be until his days are done." He looked up over his shoulder in disdain. "Her up there, she's not that kind, she's nothing special to him or anyone, and that's why she's so full of hate."

She stopped at the bottom of the stairs, not wanting to confront the family just yet.

"I'll part company with you here, Taylor, if you don't mind, and I thank you for the opinion, but I've a great deal of thinking to do."

He nodded.

"And it's best I do it alone, out on the ocean. You don't think anyone would mind if I took one of the small boats out, do you?"

His bushy brows furled and formed a straight, prickly-looking hedge over his watery eyes. "You can take a boat, right enough, and no one's to mind, but there's a blow headed for the island and I'd not like to see you caught out in it."

"I won't be long, Taylor, but I have to go. I just have to; I can't think on land."

The old man nodded, understanding well that kind of thinking. "Go on, but watch the horizon."

She had reached the boat before the sound of huffing and puffing caused her to look back.

"Where are you going?" Stavros demanded.

"I have to get away for a little while, and this seems the best way."

"Couldn't you take a walk?" he asked hopefully. "You know there's a storm coming in, Taylor said so. I don't understand why you feel you have to go out now."

No, he probably didn't, and because he didn't, she couldn't begin to explain it to him. "I'll be back hours

before the storm hits. You know I'm always careful."
She refused to be swayed by his logic, not being ruled
by that particular emotion at present.

"Rathe isn't going to like it. It's not safe," he warned.

"He isn't my keeper and he has no right to interfere
with my life, and if he asks, you can tell him I said that!"
She stormed at him and would have walked away but he
caught her arm and held it, a worried frown on his face.
"Are you sure about that, Lorelei?" he asked.

She couldn't face him with a deception. "I'm not sure
about anything Stavros, and that's why I have to go."

He handed her a bundle of clothing that had gone
unnoticed, held by his side. "Taylor said you left without
so much as a change of clothes."

"Thanks. I appreciate it." She took the offering stiffly,
just wishing he would leave and let her go.

"I'd rather lose you to him than to the storm, Lorelei,
remember that." He bit his lower lip in anguish. "I'd
rather not lose you at all. Be careful, will you, and come
back in as soon as you can?"

She kissed him full on the lips, tasting his sweetness,
trying to give back as much as she had taken. "See you
soon."

The water was rough and it provided the challenge
that she needed to clear her mind, to wipe away the
clutter of trivial detail that living on land tended to fill
her mind with. All that was important out here was keeping one's boat headed in the right direction and free of
water.

She stopped a few minutes out and switched off the
motor. Her bow was still headed out to sea, but she had
come far enough. The light rain that was falling had
obscured the hump in the distance that was Andros. It
had also soaked her to the skin. She removed the swimsuit
and sat upright in the boat, naked and gloriously alone
for the first time in weeks, allowing the misty rain to
further caress her skin. It felt good.

A few minutes later she undid the bundle of clothing

Stavros had provided and held it out with a shake of her head. A bright red wool sweater itched when she put it on over her bare breasts, but she kept it on anyway, because it was warm. The red, brown, and tan plaid wool skirt was equally impractical, but its bulky folds did cover her knees and so she left it on too, discarding the underwear in defiance of proper etiquette, along with the high-heeled sandals. Really, did he think she was going on a pleasure cruise? He had always had a different outlook, a different set of values than she did, but it hadn't mattered before now. He was gentle, affectionate, an easy companion, and not demanding at all. He had suited her needs. After Rathe had gone from her life, she had had nothing to give a more demanding man; she was an empty shell waiting to be filled, and Stavros had come along with a need for a wife and with a family full of ideas. It hadn't mattered that their ideas weren't hers, but, then, nothing had mattered much if she couldn't have Rathe.

Now things mattered. She could have him; maybe not in marriage the way, as a vulnerable eighteen-year-old, she had wanted. But she could have him, if she was willing to fight for him, and if she could get back to shore.

She noticed with a start that the storm had come in faster than she had anticipated and she had made some foolish mistakes, not the least of which was failing to keep a sharp eye on the horizon. Mother Nature was not forgiving; it hadn't been with her own mother, who had died giving birth to Lorelei at sea, and it wouldn't be with her. She had broken some cardinal rules of sailing, taught to her early by her father, and she might well have to pay dearly for her mistakes.

The motor sputtered into high and she made for the shore, riding on the back of an undulating slippery serpent bound and determined to dislodge her from her precarious position on its back and plunge her into one of the watery canyons over which cold, moving mountains of gray-green towered like giants. It might have been just such a day that the Spanish galleon met her fate, and as never before, she felt herself a kindred spirit to those ancient mariners. The sea tossed her up and down, and she, never seasick a day in her life, began to feel queasy, fear a cold lump in the bottom of her stomach.

She wasn't making the best headway, either. The gale, which had not yet hit the island in force, was still powerful enough to lift her tiny boat up and twist it around in spite of her experience, making it difficult to keep her nose perpendicular to the waves ahead and behind, forcing her to meet them broadside at times, a dangerous thing to do if she wanted to remain upright. The wind was making it even more impossible to navigate the reef in safety. Only a few feet from the surface when the sea was calm, the jagged coral fingers would be visible in the troughs, would reach out for her as they had for the galleon. She swerved this way and that, using every trick she knew to dodge the coral and find the path through its treacherous passageways, but the surf and the wind had a mind of their own and she found herself dragged over a razor-sharp vertical isthmus in spite of everything she had done to prevent it, causing a puncture in the bottom of the boat.

To be sure, the hole was not large, but the seawater was insidious, creeping with slow surety into her boat, making it ride even lower in the water than it previously had. To make matters worse, she didn't even have a cup with which to bail the water. She had only her hands, and these were fighting a rudder which threatened to snap off at any moment, no longer capable of withstanding the strain between the water and her will.

The rudder finally snapped and the motor quit simultaneously—perhaps out of gas, perhaps from too much water inside its vital parts. She didn't know, hadn't checked before leaving Andros. She hadn't been in her right mind since coming to the accursed island! However, now wasn't the time for self-recriminations. Now was the time to swim...

She closed her eyes, a fervent prayer to the god of sailors everywhere, on her lips. The boat was going down and there was no stopping it. Already tilting precariously to starboard, it lurched and settled itself even lower with a frightful gurgle, submerging itself in stages, though soon it would have no choice in the matter, and neither would she. The prospect of choosing her own time to go swimming was more appealing than waiting, her feet touching solid deck until the last vestige of security was sucked from under her, and so she readied a life preserver of sorts, rigged from the boat's buoyant cushions and tied to her body with panty hose. If she ever got to shore alive, her father would skin her alive for all the oversights, up to and including leaving land without a life preserver.

The water was inky black as she stepped into it, the makeshift life preserver holding her weight well. Resourcefulness pays off. She reminded herself of that and allowed the waves to carry her in, mindful not to expend her energy in swimming. She would need all her energy to guide herself to the proper piece of shore, to a place where the beach was comprised of sand rather than rock. She held her breath as the monstrous waves washed over her, dragging her to the bottom.

CHAPTER TWELVE

THE FIRST THING she heard upon returning to consciousness was the ocean's dull roar and the sound of rain upon the water. She looked around in consternation. Where was she? The tide moved her rhythmically back and forth, dragging her feet against the bottom . . . of what? She tested her sore muscles, found nothing broken, and attempted to stand, to climb her way out of the tide pool of seawater in which the storm had deposited her. The effort was too great and she sat down again, out of the water this time, her head resting on the cushions she was too tired to remove. She dozed in and out, not feeling the cold at all, not feeling the rain, not feeling much of anything but a curiosity as to who would find her and when. It could have been minutes later or hours when the someone she most hoped would rescue her did, lifting her from the rocks with hands warm and full of strength.

"Rathe . . . tell me it's you." She dripped against a wet jacket that smelled of fish.

"Oh, my God . . ." the man breathed, lifting her into his arms as if she were a child.

"Are we going home?" Her tongue felt swollen in her mouth and leathery and, come to think of it, gritty, and though she made a real effort to open her eyes, they refused to budge more than a crack. She looked up at him anyway, though, at his haggard, drawn features which looked wonderfully good even as they were. He'd

found her and it made her feel like singing just to have
him hold her.

"Ninety-nine bottles of rum on the wall ... ninety-
nine bottles of rum ..." It was the first tune that popped
into her head and proved once and for all that she had
no class whatsoever. Wouldn't the Halkias family be
scandalized! She grinned with cracked lips, bringing a
smile of equal size to his.

"It's beer, my dear, not rum."

"I don't like beer." Though perhaps it wasn't her
semantics he objected to, but her singing. No siren she,
and this should prove it to him. She tried an octave
higher, which didn't particularly improve the quality of
the sound: "... bring one down, pass it around ... ninety-
eight bottles of—"

"Champagne, my love. I'll personally buy you ninety-
eight bottles of champagne and help you celebrate with
each one of them if you'll just hang on until I can get
you somewhere safe."

"Are we going to go home?" she asked him again.

"No. You have a nasty cut on your head and I ... I
want to get you somewhere dry to take a look at it. We're
a long way from the plantation, too far to walk. Would
you like to go to the cave?"

"The one with the Lusca?" Her voice was hoarse from
gulping seawater. "If he decides to have me for dinner,
will you please ask him to cook me first?" She made a
poor attempt at laughter. "If I'm to die I'd much rather
do it warm. The ocean was so cold, so very cold, Rathe.
I thought I was going to die with the Spanish sailors; I
thought I'd never see you again; I thought you'd never
find me." The tears replaced the laughter and fell down,
burning her scraped cheeks.

He carried her into the opening of the cave, cradling
her with his body. "I would have found you," he said
grimly. "I haven't lost track of you in over six years and
I'm not about to lose you now."

With matches from his pocket, he started the driftwood fire in the outer cave, adding to the centuries-old layer of wood smoke that covered the ceiling and walls; and once he was sure it had started in earnest, he turned to the job of removing her clothes. Soaked and torn, they provided no comfort for her and he quickly took them from her, using the full red skirt's hem, torn in strips, for bandaging material for her head. He covered her with his jacket and brought her closer to the warming flames.

"Is the goose egg on my head as large as it feels?"

He studied the lump critically. "No. In fact you're in remarkable shape all around, all things considered. I was worried that you might have suffered a concussion... or worse, but it's a small cut, and most of the red I feared was blood, wasn't."

"It wasn't?"

"No, it wasn't. It was your dry-clean-only red wool sweater, running its magenta dye all over your skin. I've never been so relieved in my life when it washed off and there were no cuts underneath."

"You were worried?" She touched her fingers to the roughness of his cheek. "Why? Why were you worried?"

"We have been looking for you since the storm hit. We couldn't find the boat; we didn't see any signs of a wreck, no debris, no lifejacket... no you. Taylor is half out of his mind for letting you go, and so is Stavros. And now that I remember, I have to call them."

"Where are they?"

"Back at the plantation." He spoke a few sentences into the radio. "Taylor? I've found her. She's safe. Yes... yes... she's okay. No, I won't risk drenching her again. We'll see you in the morning. Send Stavros as far as you can in the jeep, but don't try it until daylight. The storm surf is too high right now." He turned the radio off.

"You continued looking for me after the others had gone." She watched him curiously. "Why?"

"We both know the answer to that. And, too, I felt more responsible than anyone for you being out there.

This hot-and-cold war of ours hasn't been easy."

"I was at war with myself, not with you. We don't have to fight anymore, Rathe." She held his attention with the unmistakable message.

The hands holding both her shoulders tightened their grip. "You don't mean what I think you're trying to say. You're grateful to be alive, but a simple 'thank you, Rathe, and I won't be so stupid next time,' will do."

"Will it?"

"I wouldn't want to be accused of taking advantage of you in the morning, and there are still the other ...commitments. You know that."

He was warning her that Carmen still played a big part in his life. It was a gamble she would have to take. She loved him enough to fight for him. "I came very close tonight to sharing a bed with Neptune at the bottom of the sea. I made a promise to myself, that if I ever got to dry land again, I would share a bed with you." She unfastened the buttons of his jacket which she wore, very slowly, two, three, four, until the closures fell open to reveal the soft roundness of her body within. She slipped the material off one shoulder and shrugged it off the other, allowing the garment to fall behind at her feet. The firelight lent a warm glow to her arms as she held them out to him.

"Love me." She whispered the plea.

Rathe exhaled loudly and didn't say anything at all, whatever reservations he had had seemingly swept from his mind. He drew her nearer and allowed her to remove his own wet shirt, helping her as she fumbled with the belt at his waist.

The touch of his hands on her skin was electrifying as he sought to drive away the cold that was making her shiver, massaging her tense muscles with his fingers, slowly reviving her half-frozen extremities. He moved his hands from the tips of her cold-stiffened nipples, down the goose-pimpled belly, and lower still, until the warmth of life had returned to her, until she moaned with the heat of her desire and arched her hips to seek his. Her passion was mirrored in his own body as he knelt beside her, his need controlled and contained no longer.

"There is no turning back now, sweet siren—know that! You are mine." His eyes met hers in silent promise as he pulled her to him and lowered them both to the ground, his clothes a bed upon which they lay, an altar on which they worshipped each other with their hands, their lips, and more. . . . He had found her, she held him close, and all the furies of wind and sea that raged in an ever-increasing, deafening crescendo outside were not enough to part them, to prevent them from becoming one with each other and renewing the love they had once lost, and had never thought to regain.

The crackling of an open fire interrupted the sweet dreams that had comforted her during the night and she closed her eyes tightly to recapture them before remembering. . . . There was no need to hold on to the company of dreams when there was the warm reality to hold, right next to her. She rolled over to find Rathe. He was gone.

"So you are awake at last? You gave everyone quite a scare last night with your antics. They were afraid you might not wake up again at all."

"Carmen?" Her eyes flew open in surprise. "What are you doing here?" She sat up and slipped into Rathe's warm jacket.

Carmen leaned against the stone wall of the cave. She looked rumpled and bored. "I'm baby-sitting—or discharging an obligation to Rathe, if you prefer."

"Where is Rathe?" The sun was high in the sky, the space next to her cold. He had been absent for some time.

The deep, full red lips were parted in a sneer. "Back at the plantation where I wish I was, though I can see why he wanted me to keep a sharp eye on you."

"You aren't making any sense, Carmen." She sat up suddenly, too suddenly, her head spinning with the effort. "Rathe asked you to keep an eye on me?"

"You don't really think I'd be here, keeping you company, if he hadn't asked me to, do you?"

She could see the truth in that. Carmen seldom left Rathe's side unless pried from it forcibly.

"Are you saying something to her? You were supposed to come get us when she woke up. If you've upset her—" Sarah stormed into the cave, dropping an armload of driftwood next to the fire.

"It's okay, Sarah." Stavros followed her in. "It's been hard on all of us. I'm sure Carmen wasn't upsetting anyone." He poured a cup of tea from an aluminum pot balanced precariously on the coals and brought it over, helping her sit up to drink it.

"How do you feel?" He smoothed back a strand of her hair, careful not to dislodge the bandages on her head.

"Better, I think. Rathe said it didn't look too bad last night." She pulled the wraps off to let him have a look.

Sarah swallowed a gasp. "Do you want some aspirin? I brought some along just in case." She stepped closer to inspect the cut. "I hope you like purple."

"And black and blue." Stavros winced in empathy. "It looks a lot better than I imagined though; it's just a small cut. We were all imagining things much worse; even Rathe was shaken up." He lowered his voice confidentially. "Carmen, too. When he radioed that he had found you, she all but begged us to bring you in with the jeep, she was that worried."

"And you should have seen mama, searching the shoreline in her curlers and red-flannel nightie." Sarah knelt beside Stavros, blue circles marring the fair complexion under her eyes. "I was so worried."

"We all were, and we're very glad you're all right." He buttoned the jacket up tighter. "I don't want you to catch cold."

"Oh, honestly!" Carmen tossed the tin teacup to the sand. "She wasn't drowned, she was wet. And while we're at it, before you welcome home the prodigal son, don't you think we'd better ask her where the gold is?"

"Drop it, Carmen." Stavros was stern.

"Drop what?" She met each of their eyes only to find she could outstare them all except Carmen. "She's been dying to tell me something since I woke up, and I don't know what it is, but I think we should stop trying to coddle me and tell me what it is."

"It's just this," Carmen boasted triumphant. "Last night while everyone else was weeping and wailing and hunting for our lost comrade, contrary to the story Stavros told you, I was back at the plantation. I happened to go into the artifact room, and lo and behold, Rathe's gold artifacts were gone."

"Gone? Gone? What do you mean by *gone?* Had they been moved?"

"Gone, Lorelei dear, as in *without permission*. I think the word is *stolen*. And isn't it odd that the only person to leave the island since the reporters were thrown off is you, and that your boat is conveniently missing? Wrecked, so you say, though we have no evidence of that and you don't look too much the worse for wear—as you would if you were really shipwrecked in a storm like that."

She stood up stiffly and hobbled to within inches of Carmen, her very bones aching with the battering they had received. "Are you accusing me of stealing? I'd trade bodies even with you this morning, Carmen. I was lucky to get into shore with my hide. I don't have even my own clothing, much less any of Rathe's artifacts."

"No? Then where did you get the necklace? A local five-and-dime?"

"My necklace?" Her hands flew to the present at her neck. Now was not the time to get into who had given her the gift and why, yet she couldn't think of anything to say that would prevent Carmen from going on with the questions.

"It's an artifact," the other woman continued. "And

it's one that I haven't seen. Either you found it and kept it, which is stealing, since everything from the *Princess* belongs to Poseidon Enterprises; someone else found it and you took it, which is the same; or Rathe gave it to you..." She touched the stone. "It is a very valuable bauble to give one's employee—genuine amethyst and gold, six or seven hundred dollars' worth of jewelry easy, even without the antique considerations. It's the kind of present one might give to a loved one, the kind of gift a man might give his mistress, don't you think so, Stavros?" She whirled on Stavros and Sarah, contemplating their confusion with satisfaction.

"How I got the necklace doesn't really concern you, Carmen, and since you don't have any proof of your accusations, I hope you won't repeat them." It was a lukewarm defense, but she feared that losing her temper would only lend credence to the remarks. "Right now I'm going to find Rathe. I want to get this thing cleared up as soon as I can. You say he's back at the plantation?"

"So he said. But a word to the wise: I wouldn't cross his path just now if I were you. He's pretty angry."

"I don't believe he thinks I'm guilty."

Carmen stretched and shrugged. "Believe what you like. It would suit me fine if you went back—then I could go back too. But as to him believing you guilty—I'm sure he doesn't want to, but it's just that there's so much evidence against you, don't you see? The smashed vase, the reporters, and now this. It was a crushing blow and he left as soon as I told him...he didn't want to stay here any longer with you."

"And what did you tell him, Carmen?" There was a cutting edge to Stavros's question, foreign to his usual tolerant nature.

"I don't think you really want to know," she answered him flippantly.

"Perhaps not, but I think you'd better tell me anyway."

She walked to the mouth of the cave. "I found them sleeping together, your fiancé and mine, this morning before you arrived. I simply pointed out that it was a little too convenient, her giving in to his demands last night, after denying him for the past weeks. If she hadn't, he would have come back to the plantation, I feel sure of it. He would have discovered the gold was missing in time to do something about it, maybe. Now, for all he knows, his gold could be at the bottom of the sea, or more likely in the hands of whomever she's working with. I simply pointed out to him that she could have used . . . last night . . . as a means to gain his trust . . . to win his affection so that the suspicion wouldn't land at her feet."

"That's a perfectly awful thing to say, and you *don't* have any proof. It's just your word against hers, and I'm taking her word." Sarah protected her friend fiercely.

"It's more than that. It's her word against ours . . . . Rathe's and mine. If it weren't, why would he call her father to come fetch her?"

"My father?" What had he to do with anything?

"I said Rathe wants you off this island," Carmen hissed. "And he wants you off badly enough to call your father to come and get you."

Lorelei reached out to Stavros for support. "Is she telling the truth?" Her heart begged that it not be so.

"Yes, she's telling the truth." Sarah wrung her hands anxiously. "At least, Rathe said he was going to call him to come for you. He sent us out here with a change of clothes for you and breakfast, with instructions that we stay put until he came back. He didn't explain why."

"He's called my father." She couldn't believe that, not after all they had shared. "What else? What else did he say?" She had to know the rest. "Does he think I stole the gold? Does he think I'm working with his pirates? Does he really think I made love with him last night as a diversion?" She clamped a hand over her mouth, too late. She had meant to give the engagement ring back to Stavros today, to explain, if she could, what had happened, privately. She had wanted to leave him his pride.

Now she had taken herself from him, and his honor as well.

"I don't think he believes any of that, Lorelei." Stavros didn't look surprised, or perhaps he was choosing not to look surprised, to put a damper on Carmen's gloating.

"And if she has convinced him of it, we'll change his mind. No one else believes you capable of any of that." Sarah handed her a change of clothes. "Here, put these on and we'll all go talk to him."

"Count me out for your list of character witnesses. I know the truth about you," Carmen said, the hatred in her eyes matching that in her voice.

Lorelei crawled back into the inner chamber and hastily changed into the black cowl-necked sweater, skintight blue jeans, and tennis shoes that Sarah had given her. Carmen's story did have a small grain of truth. She had given herself to Rathe last night, given the sum total of herself in the hopes that she would win his love and his trust. But she had failed and she had nothing more to give him. If he did not believe in her innocence now, all the talking she or her loyal followers could do would not change his mind; and he had made up his mind. For him to call her father to come for her, he would have to believe her guilty. There was nothing for her to do but go, with as much or as little pride still left to her. Her only hope was that she could leave before he had to throw her, figuratively, off the island, before she had to see the disillusionment in his face that only seemed to grow bigger the harder she tried to dispel it.

She left the smaller chamber and made her way to the outside. "I'm going to take a boat and leave Andros now, before my father gets here. I will be in Nassau if Rathe needs to get in touch with me."

"You can't leave," Sarah cried woefully. "For one thing, there isn't a boat available that I'd trust in a storm like this."

"Except Rathe's," Carmen interjected silkily. "She's

taken everything else from him, why not that as well?"

"Shut up, Carmen." Sarah was almost in tears.

"That's not a bad idea." Lorelei snapped the amethyst pendant from her neck and let the beautiful object dangle between her fingers for a long moment before handing it over to Sarah. "Give this to Rathe, will you? Tell him I said it was for the rental of his boat. I will have it returned to him by tomorrow night."

She walked slowly from the cave, squinting as the harsh sunlight struck her eyes. The way she felt, she would have preferred to spend the day . . . the week . . . inside the dark womb of the cavern, but the reason for staying had gone, and he had taken her heart with him.

"Lorelei, don't go." Stavros stopped her slow but determined flight and swung her around to meet his eyes, a thing she hadn't been able to force herself to do. "Look at me. . . . Look . . . at . . . me. I'm telling you the same thing that I told you yesterday. It's not safe to sail today and I don't want you out on the water. Why, you can barely stand; you certainly can't navigate in this kind of weather. Do you think I've searched all night for you only to let you go and do the same stupid thing again?"

"I should think you'd be glad to get rid of me. I have to go anyway. Rathe wants me to go. You heard Carmen, and if you don't believe her, you heard Sarah. Surely you'll believe Sarah. I don't have a choice about whether I go, Stavros, only about when I go and in what transportation. Please don't take that option from me, Stavros."

"I'm not trying to take anything away from you, Lorelei. All I have ever wanted to do was give to you." He moved to embrace her. "And now I see that the best thing I can give to you, my beautiful, beautiful lady, is your freedom to deal with Rathe, to settle what lies between you and find happiness." At her tear-filled look of surprise he continued. "He's the person who finally bridged the wall to your heart. I was never able to; and that is fair, in its way, because he is the one responsible for building that wall. Don't you think it fair that he be the one to tear it down?"

She thought that her past with Rathe was a well-guarded secret. "How did you know about us?"

He walked with her up the beach, oblivious to the foamy waves that dashed around their feet. "I don't know very much, only that there was a man in your past who hurt you terribly. Your father told me that, but I had suspected it before. I know you much better than you think I do. I've known since coming to Andros that Rathe is the man in your past, just as I knew he would be the man in your future."

"My future will *not* be on Andros, Stavros. You know, I felt it was a mistake to come here. I felt it that first day. It's too bad I didn't listen to my own intuition."

The docks and Rathe's sloop tied up along the side of them loomed up ahead. "I want you to find happiness, Lorelei, and if you cannot find it with me, then please, find it with Rathe Drummond. Don't run away from it again."

"I don't know if that's possible. The way things look, I won't be able to find happiness with either of you."

He sat down upon the wooden dock planks. "Such an all-or-nothing, intense woman you are," he sighed. "Let me tell you something, something Greek; perhaps I can explain myself to you. There is more to the emotion of love than what you Americans see on television or what you read about in the romantic novels; more depth, more variation, more forgiveness. . . . There are as many kinds of love as there are people. I, for instance, will still love you, always, even though our relationship will not be the same as we intended. Nothing can change my feelings for you, or, I suspect, your feelings for me. It is the same for you and Rathe. The problems you had in the past did not keep you from loving him, eh? Or keep him from loving you. Whether you go or you stay, you will still feel the same, both of you. So why not stay, so we will not all have to worry about you?"

She had listened to him. "I am glad that we can be friends. I'll be needing all the friends I can get. But I'm afraid Rathe isn't a product of your Greek upbringing, and he doesn't share your Greek philosophy. In his kind of love, there is no room for forgiveness, at least not for the things he believes I have done." She slipped the diamond engagement ring from her finger and pressed it in his palm. "I hope you find someone worthy to wear it. You are a special, wonderful man . . ." She kissed him good-bye.

CHAPTER THIRTEEN

LORELEI CLIMBED ABOARD Rathe's sloop and turned her back on Andros, her bow pointed toward New Providence and the peace of mind she'd left behind. Suddenly she heard a thud behind her and she turned—there would be no easy escape for her, she realized, for standing on the deck of the ship was Rathe, and Stavros was no longer in sight.

"Just where do you think you're going, woman?" he asked.

"Where you want me to—away from this cursed island," she responded. "You should be glad I'm following your wishes for once."

He reached her side and caught her arm. "Don't worry," she assured him before he could speak, "I'm not making off with any of your precious gold—that's just another story your fiancée made up. The fool. To think she actually believed she'd have to say something to come between us..."

Lorelei broke off as she realized that Rathe's gray eyes were not full of anger, as she had thought, but of something that looked like concern.

"Of course I know you don't have the gold, Lorelei. Lucy just found it—stashed away in Carmen's room. Carmen never was that much of a housekeeper, but I guess that sand all over the floor made Lucy suspicious. All she had to do was open the closet door." Then his face darkened. "But where in the world did you ever get the idea that she was my fiancée?"

"She told me."

He sighed, exasperated. "When I first met Carmen, she was a vivacious, independent, lovely woman, and I had shut myself off from living for quite a while. We worked well together. She is a very professional photographer. On a social level—" He shrugged, admitting but not apologizing for his past. "I'm no saint, Lorelei, but I had no legal ties to anyone else and neither did she. She wasn't interested, any more than I, in forming a permanent relationship, at first. I told her point-blank that I was in love with another woman, that I would always be in love with another woman. I thought she accepted it... until she met the other woman!"

Lorelei should have known that a man like Rathe would have more than one woman in his past, but the knowledge hurt nonetheless. "I'm sorry. It must have been terribly hard for you, finding out about the gold."

"And the rest. I owe you an apology—for the vase, the reporters. She was responsible for that too. I couldn't see it before..." He looked hard at her. Then he began to speak, in soft, husky low tones, pouring out all the emotion she hadn't believed him capable of feeling.

"As I said before, I owe you apology after apology. I didn't think you took my gold, and certainly I didn't think you seduced me for less than honorable reasons last night." He nibbled at her neck. "Though you *did* seduce me, little sea witch. I owe you the apology because I, at one time, thought you might be responsible for the smashed vase and the reporters coming to the island. I should have known you wouldn't have done that."

She could feel his chest contract and expand against her back as he took several preparing breaths.

"I... have been angry at you for a long time, for preferring Stavros over me. I came up with a hundred and one reasons why you might have said no to my proposal six years ago, all of them wrong. You are not promiscuous, or on the other end of the spectrum, or security-seeking, or any of the other things I intimated. I needed to find a reason why you had not chosen to be with me; I needed a reason to hate you, since you refused to let me love you. Later, when you came to Andros, I thought Carmen had provided me with that reason— the vase, the reporters. By the time I realized she had implicated you out of her own jealousy, you had run from me again..."

"I wasn't ever running away from you." He had been painfully frank with her about his feelings; she could throw her minute bit of pride away and do the same for him. "I was running away from myself. I cared for Stavros deeply, I still do, but every time you came near me, I wanted you, I loved you, even more than I had as a girl. It frightened me. I wanted to be a man's wife, not his mistress. It came to me, yesterday, when I was in the water, trying to get to shore, that I would be a thousand times happier as your mistress than I would be as Stavros's wife." She looked away from him shyly. "I know that you don't want more, that there is some other woman in your past that you still love and for some reason can't have; but if you want me to, for as long as you want me to, I will be your mistress."

"*My mistress!* You think I want you only as my lover?" His incredulity was like a slap on her face.

"Don't sound so shocked. I thought you'd be *pleased* I was finally following your orders ... for a change."

"Lorelei, if I could have ordered you to become anything to me, I would have done it years ago." He gathered her into his arms. "*You* are the woman in my past whom I shall always love, and believe me, I never wanted you as my mistress—I wanted you for my wife. But you didn't want me. Even so, I couldn't seem to let you go. I followed your tour boat around the islands for years; I came to your engagement party to see if there was still time to change your mind. When I saw that I was too late, I came up with the idea of hiring Stavros to come to work for me . . . I'll admit it, yes, to part you."

"But I came too."

"You did, and you didn't want anything to do with me on Andros either. It drove me crazy trying to devise ways to keep you two apart and us together." He paused uncomfortably. "I like Stavros Halkias. But I love you with all my being. I *don't* love you enough to let you go back to him. You are mine; I told you that last night before I took you to my bed, and I meant it." He frowned in contemplation. "I wonder if I could hire a minister to marry us right away?"

"I haven't said yes yet, Mr. Drummond."

"You will . . ." he warned. "Or I won't let you leave this island."

"Such drastic measures won't be necessary. I didn't know how you felt before, but now that I do, nothing on heaven or earth will keep me from you. There is no other man on earth for me." She kissed him with a fervor that came from deep within her, fanning a fire too long banked. Their embrace deepened, their bodies pressed together, heedless of anything except the love between them that had finally been expressed in words as well as acts.

"Oh, my siren," Rathe said roughly, looking into her sea-deep green eyes, "I'll never let you go again."

Lorelei was exultant. And as his lips met hers, her body arching back to take his full embrace, the pain of the years they had lost melted away.

Introducing a unique new concept in romance novels!
Every woman deserves a…

Second Chance at Love™

™
You'll revel in the settings, you'll delight
in the heroines, you may even fall in love with the
magnetic men you meet in the pages of…

SECOND CHANCE AT LOVE

Look for three new
novels of lovers lost and found coming every
month from Jove! Available now: